Also by Olivia Gaines

Modern Mail Order Brides

On A Rainy Night in Georgia

Buckeye and the Babe

The Tennessee Mountain Man

Bleu, Grass, Bourbon

Serenity Series

Welcome to Serenity

Holden

Farmer Takes A Wife

Slice of Life

Friends with Benefits

Slivers of Love

The Cost to Play

Thursdays in Savannah

The Blakemore Files

Being Mrs. Blakemore
Shopping with Mrs. Blakemore
Dancing with Mr. Blakemore
Cruising with the Blakemores
Dinner with the Blakemores
Loving the Czar
Being Mr. Blakemore
A Weekend with the Blakemores

The Davonshire Series
Courting Guinevere

The Men of Endurance
A Walk Through Endurance
Intervals of Love
The Art of Persistence
A Walk Through Endurance

The Value of A Man
My Mail Order Wife
A Weekend with the Cromwells
Cutting it Close

Standalone
Santa's Big Helper
A Menu For Loving
North to Alaska
Turning the Page

An Untitled Love
Wyoming Nights
Montana
Blind Date
The Christmas Quilts

Watch for more at ogaines.com.

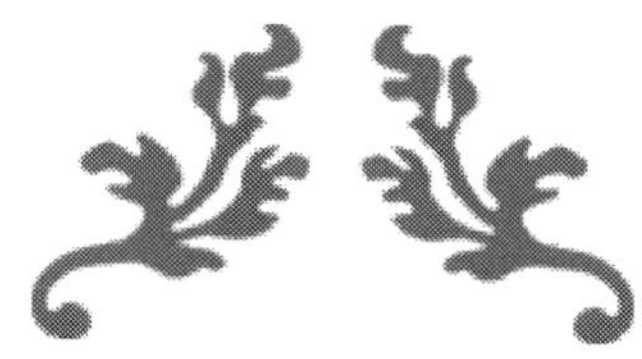

The Tennessee Mountain Man

Olivia Gaines

NOVEMBER 19, 2018
DAVONSHIRE HOUSE PUBLISHING
Hephzibah, Georgia

Davonshire House Publishing
PO Box 9716
Augusta, GA 30916

THIS BOOK IS A WORK of fiction. Names, characters, places, and incidents are products of the author's vivid imagination or are used fictitiously. Any resemblance to actual events, locales or persons, living or dead, is entirely a coincidence.

Copy Editor: Teri Thompson Blackwell

Cover: Nu Class Graphicz

Olivia Gaines Make Up and Photograph by Latasla Gardner Photography

ASIN: B077RJFG3W

Printed in the United States of America

1 2 3 4 5 6 7 10 9 8

First Davonshire House Publishing February 2018

DEDICATION

For Teri.

Sometimes I get it right on the onset, when I don't, that is why I have you.

"Easy reading is damn hard writing."

- Nathaniel Hawthorne

ACKNOWLEDGMENTS

A special thank you to the Tuesday Sushi Club, Jessica, and Hildie, for keeping me grounded.

To all the fans, friends and supporters of the dream as well as the Facebook community of writers who keep me focused, inspired and moving forward.

Write On!

[1]

1. https://www.facebook.com/theauthormag

Also by Olivia Gaines

THE SLICE OF LIFE SERIES

- The Perfect Man
- Friends with Benefits
- A Letter to My Mother
- The Basement of Mr. McGee
- A New Mommy for Christmas

The Slivers of Love Series

- The Cost to Play
- Thursday in Savannah
- Girl's Weekend
- Beneath the Well of Dawn
- Santa's Big Helper

The Davonshire Series

- Courting Guinevere
- Loving Words
- Vanity's Pleasure

The Blakemore Files

- Being Mrs. Blakemore
- Shopping with Mrs. Blakemore
- Dancing with Mr. Blakemore
- Cruising with the Blakemores
- Dinner with the Blakemores
- Loving the Czar

The Value of a Man Series

- My Mail Order Wife
- A Weekend with the Cromwell's

Other Novellas

- North to Alaska
- The Brute & The Blogger
- A Better Night in Vegas

Other Novels

- A Menu for Loving
- Turning the Page

Chapter One – Worst Week Ever

Chicago, Illinois

Khloe Burgess sat on her front porch, the smoldering embers crackling behind her while the ache in her head thumped and angry blood pumped into the grey matter. Disbelief overcame any attempt to get on her feet and get moving because honestly, she didn't know what to say, what to do, or how to even respond to just one more situation that she labeled as the worst week ever. It was only Wednesday. The week wasn't even over yet.

People walked by, asking if she was okay. The furthest thing from her mind was whether or not she was okay. From where she sat, shit would never be okay again in her life ever. And it was only Wednesday.

The previous Sunday morning, before her shift at Mercy Memorial Hospital in Chicago where she held a glorified position as a Nurse Practitioner, three thugs had chased her during her morning run. Luckily, the idiots were sagging their pants, which hindered their ability to catch up to her to do whatever dastardly deed had entered their small minds. She had escaped one horrific fate only to enter her workplace and be shot at by the wife of Dr. Lombardi, the resident male whore who found it necessary to hump every woman willing to spread her legs. His latest conquest, believing her love affair with the roaming Romeo made her special, then took it upon herself to call his wife. The sad part was that as emboldened as Nurse Vicky believed herself to be, she wasn't courageous enough to give Nancy Lombardi her real name. Instead, Vicky decided to tell Nancy that her name was Khloe Burgess.

The bullet from the gun, held by a shaky Nancy, went into the wall. Dr. Lombardi, in his effort to wrestle the gun away from his enraged wife, ended up with a gut shot. Khloe, ashamed of her own thoughts, wished the shot had hit the man a bit lower. He was a disgusting man, who by any standards wasn't even good looking, and had an average penis. This she knew for a fact since she'd caught him in the on-call room several times in a state of readiness with different young women. The man, whose first name was Roger, was a menace that walked around all day tugging his penis.

"I need a new life. This one sucks," Khloe remarked as she applied pressure to the bullet wound in his belly while others prepared Roger Lombardi for surgery.

It wasn't a normal day at the office. Nothing in her life this week was normal, but tomorrow was her day off. A day away from the hospital with sick people only to spend it with her mother, who made people sick. Especially Khloe, but it was Monday. A new day.

"Morning Mom," she said cheerfully as she entered the childhood home she and her brother Dorian had grown up in. The house smelled of sour beer and old cigarette smoke trapped in the walls and pissy carpet. The status of the carpet came by way of her mother, who was on another drinking binge.

"Don't morning me. Don't say good morning either, cause ain't a goddamn thing good about it," Erica Burgess slurred. "Where is that peasy headed brother of yours? He doesn't even come by anymore to check on his Momma."

"I'm here, Mom," she said, getting the woman off the floor. From the way her mother was sprawled on the floor, it appeared as if she'd spent the better part of the night there, soaked in her own waste. "Let's get you to the shower."

"I ain't your damned child!"

"Then stop shitting on yourself like you are, Mom," Khloe said, reaching for her mother but not moving fast enough to avoid the swing of the woman's fist, which made contact with her eye.

This was the way it normally went, but usually, Khloe moved fast enough to duck from the wayward swings. "Mom, I'm going to have to put you in a home," Khloe said. "You can't be left alone."

"Then I will live with you," Erica said.

"Mom, I don't know why you hate me so much to suggest such a thing," she said softly, trying again to get her mother on her feet without getting the caked-on fecal matter on her own. "Something has to give. We can't keep doing this."

"You may not be able to, but I can. I will drink as long as I can get my hands on a bottle," Erica said. "Ricky is a son of a bitch who left me with all of this. Two kids. A mortgage and a dog I didn't even like. You know that fucker bit me?"

"Yes Mom, I do," Khloe said somberly as she got the thin woman into the stand-up shower. Ricky Burgess left them when Khloe was five and Dorian was eight. Thirty-two years later, her mother was still drinking and blaming the man for not wanting to come home every day to a woman who smelled like pee, Kool Menthols, and another man. The sad part was that he left his children with her as well. For many years she held a cool resentment for the man she called father. The one year turned into five and before she knew it, her childhood had ended. It was time to be an adult and head into the adult world.

On Khloe's 18th birthday, she had joined the Army and trained as a nurse. Time again flew past and 20 years, seven countries, and two wars later, she returned to Chicago to do good by her community. Too bad the community didn't want to do good by her.

Tuesday morning, Khloe spotted Paddington Clawfoot, her Rottweiler, walking down the street with the local drug dealer. She whistled for the dog to come to her side but the animal looked at her and continued on with his new master. She was uncertain if the protector she'd raised from a pup to be her bodyguard was stolen or if he too had become tired of her lonely life. The dog had no intention of coming back and she sure as hell wasn't about to get confrontational with a drug dealer, so she let it be.

Opening her front door, she realized why the dog had left. Her mother was in her house. How the woman managed to consistently get in, even after she'd had the locks changed and a security system installed, befuddled her. Today, Khloe felt like Paddington Clawfoot. She wanted to get the hell out of that house as well.

"Mom, what are you doing here?"

"You said I didn't need to live alone, so I am going to move in with you," Erica said with glassy eyes.

"No, you aren't, Mom," she said.

"Well, just let me stay tonight until you get off shift," her mother said. "Your damned dog tried to bite me, so I burned him with a cigarette and kicked his black ass out!"

"He was my dog and you had no right," Khloe said. "How did you get in my house anyway?'

"Joey let me in," Erica said with pride.

"Why was Joey in my house?" she asked, concerned, going past her mother to her bedroom to check the jewelry box. Joseph Greenwood, her on again, off again boyfriend, aka Joey Montana, the poker player, had a nasty habit. He gambled. For every hot streak, he had one more that was tepid. Joey would win big and buy expensive baubles and trinkets for Khloe, then hit a low point and come to take it all back.

"I assume you two had some hot loving planned for this morning," her mother said, standing in the middle of the floor with urine running down her leg.

"Mom! Seriously?"

"What?"

"I can't with you today. I just can't," Khloe said, looking into the jewelry box and spying all the empty slots where her boyfriend had ripped her off. Again. It was a constant cycle of crazy and she wanted off the "Ferris Wheel of Stupid."

"Don't tell me what you can and can't do! I am your mother for Christ's sake," she slurred.

"Don't bring Jesus into this unless you plan to give your wretched soul to him for salvation," Khloe mumbled. She regretted the words but she would speak to her mother in the morning when she returned from her shift at the hospital. It was just Tuesday. The week had only officially begun.

Wednesday morning, tired, ready to face her mother's antics, she returned home to find her house in a pile of ashes, and a charred body on a gurney being wheeled out. Everything she owned had been in the house. All of it burned to black soot. No clothes. Not even a pot to piss in or a window to toss it out of was left. She stood as the body rolled past her, unable to cry, robbed of all feeling, even one of relief.

"Miss, you live here?" the Fire Chief asked.

"I did," she said softly. "What happened?"

"From what I could tell, the fire started in the back bedroom. Looks like a bottle of booze was on the floor, and whoever that was in there fell asleep with a cigarette, it caught a bit of paper on fire and the whole thing went up like kindling," the Fire Chief said. "Miss, can you identify the woman on the gurney?"

"She was my mother, Erica Burgess," Khloe said.

"I'm sorry for your loss," he told her.

In some sense of the universe giving her a pass in an effort to ensure her sanity, she too was sorry for the loss. Truthfully, she'd never known the Erica Burgess that a dude named Ricky fell in love with and married. At some point, when her life made sense, she would reach out to the man and find out where it went south. Behaviors, as she was once told by a commanding officer, are formed out of the necessity to protect the mind from damage. Even if the damage done to the body is as great as what is done to the soul.

Her mother had rotted both her body and her soul. Khloe didn't want to think it, but the idea just kind of showed up in her head. Her mother's body was filled with enough alcohol to make the woman a piece of kindling. The dull throb in her temples made her want to lie down for the rest of the week.

It was just Wednesday. She sat on what remained of her front porch and looked at the fire engines all shiny and red, with flashing lights. The trucks pulled off, leaving her alone in misery until she got to her feet and drove herself to the old house that smelled of urine, stale cigarettes and sadness.

Letting herself into the house, she trudged her way to the old bedroom where she often hid in the back closet when her mother's drunken friends would come calling. Staring at the ceiling, she tried to find the tears, but they just wouldn't flow. Later.

"Later, I will call Dorian, but right now, I just want to sleep," she said, closing her eyes and drifting off into one of the more peaceful slumbers she'd had in years.

HARBUCK, TENNESSEE

Beauregard "Beau" Montgomery sat in the back of the church watching one Hannah Bryndle say "*I Do*" to a mush-mouth, meat-mangler named Marty Manchester. He didn't know which irritated him more, that the woman dumped him for a tenderfoot named Marty, or that she was marrying the slack-jawed meat processor who short-changed old people on the only meat that could be hunted in these parts.

"Dude, why did you come if you gon' sit here giving' em the evil eye?" his cousin Jethro asked.

"I came to wish them well," Beauregard said.

"Do ya?"

"Do I what?"

"Wish' em well?" Jethro asked.

"Yep," he said. "If there are any two people in this world who deserve each other, it's them two ass wipes."

"You know what I heard?" Jethro asked, staring at his large cousin. He sat there, his green eyes twinkling, the shock of red hair sticking high on his head like a cowlick on acid, blinking at Beauregard, who sat waiting.

"Jethro, do you expect me to pull it out your head or are you gonna tell me?"

"Oh, yeah," Jethro said as if remembering the thought that had popped into that head of his. "I heard that she slept with his cousin last week and the two of them, her and the cousin, plan to rob ole Marty blind."

"Heard that, too," Beau said.

"You believe it?"

"With those two snakes, you can believe almost anything you hear," he said, frowning in distaste at the overly loud tongue kissing. His stomach lurched and he got to his feet, making others in the church turn to look at him. He offered a half-hearted wave to the crowd and skedaddled out of the building.

"Beau! Hey Beau! Wait up," Jethro yelled, coming after him in a hurry. "Wanted to tell you something."

The large man, known for his patience of a saint, arm tattoos, and large, imposing stature stood, in his best pair of dress pants, nice shoes, and a tie, waiting for his cousin to remember whatever in the hell he wanted to say.

"Jethro, these shoes are pinching my toes," he offered to his cousin.

"Oh yeah," Jethro said. "Maybe you should go home and change."

Beau pressed his lips together and counted to ten, hoping that lightning didn't strike him in the nuts for wanting to kick the shit out of Jethro. "I was going to change, but you stopped me. Remember? You said you wanted to tell me something," he emphasized, speaking slowly.

"Oh yeah, I wanted to tell you something," Jethro said, arching his furry eyebrows.

"Will it be today, Jethro?"

His cousin, an odd man with a weird sense of communication skills, leaned back in the wing tips and offered him a full-toothed smile. Jethro had a dental plan as he proudly informed everyone he met while he showed off his very healthy set of chompers.

"Oh yeah!" Jethro said with a grin. "I was down in Huntsville, Alabama last week and met a fella by the name of Roscoe. You know like, Roscoe P. Coletrain of the Dukes of Hazard? Well, he up and got himself a wife."

"And that impacts me how, Jethro?'

"He used one of them mail order bride services out of New York. Roscoe was pleased as punch with himself because he said that service matches you up with the ideal mate, not a wife, but mate," he said. "You have to take this test, give blood, urine, and I think a poop sample, too, just to make sure your kids won't come out with one leg shorter than the other and a funny eye."

"Dear Lord man, is there a point to this?" Beau asked.

"Oh yeah, I wanted to tell you something," Jethro said.

"Gosh dang it, would you fucking tell me already!"

"You should use the service, too," Jethro said.

"What? Beauregard Montgomery don't need any help with the ladies," he said with pride.

"Ladies, no. A wife, yes," Jethro said. "You got some funny ways about you, Beau."

Beau stood on the sidewalk, glaring at his cousin while his shoes seemed to shrink around his toes. At this point, Beau was uncertain if the shoes or the conversation with Jethro was causing the most pain.

"Hear me out," Jethro said. "We could sure use a doctor or even a Nurse Practitioner in these parts, 'specially for our kin. Maybe...now think about this...you oughta get you one of them brides."

"You came to this conclusion all by yourself?"

"I ain't no dummy, Beauregard Montgomery," Jethro said defiantly. "But you are if you think some woman is going to willingly live on that mountain, growing her own vegetables, drinking pulverized cabbage mixed with strawberries as a breakfast drink, then you're wrong. The way I see it, you can place an ad, pay the fee, and find you a lady bear to hibernate with this winter. You know, make a few more Montgomery's while you're at it."

"Jethro, you are saying that you think I'm weird?"

"Your word, cuz, not mine, but I don't know many ladies who want to spend the evening reading about dragon queens sleeping with their nephew then watching the show on pay per watch television," Jethro said. "Plus, you have different tastes. What you like to dine on ain't served much in these parts."

"Goodbye Jethro," Beau said, walking away.

"Beau, this is a win-win for you, the community, and a weird bear-loving woman who's just waiting for you to come find her," Jethro said. "Wait up. I have the number for the matchmaking woman in New York."

He didn't know why, but Beauregard accepted the number. After making it home and ridding himself of the toe-pinching shoes, another force outside of himself made him call the nice lady in New York. Caroline Newair, that was her name and she wanted to meet him in person. Well, that was after he heard Caroline Newair clicking away on her computer with each statement, he made about himself. He'd figured she was looking him up and doing a background check on him.

New York. He'd been a few times himself in college, then one for a football game. Beau didn't much care for the place or the millions of people who lived in such confined space. But, a mate would be nice.

"I'd love to meet you as well," he said, using his college-mock-interview-for-a-job voice.

Then, for the dimmest reason, he called Billy Joe Remmer, who flew planes for the drug cartel. As far as he could tell, Joey made weekly runs to New York, Vermont, and sometimes Philadelphia. Luck was on his side and tomorrow, the plane was headed for the Big Apple. The apple had worms but he was going anyway and before he knew it, he was in New York.

That Monday afternoon, he found himself in the offices of Perfect Match, having a conversation with one and the same green-eyed Coraline Newair who reminded him of a witch. Beauregard learned two things that day. One, he could crap on command because the lady did, in fact, take a poop sample and two, Jethro wasn't as stupid as he acted.

It took several tries to get the ad right and he wasn't satisfied, but the nice lady said he had time. She needed to fly back with him to Tennessee and see his home and business and meet his folks. It was fine by him because Billy Joe Remmer wasn't coming back for an extraction and Beau needed to way back home.

Beau wasn't an idiot either. The Coraline woman wanted the time alone on the flight with him to pick his brain and get to know him better. That part he appreciated. The hefty $10,000 fee he had to pay, not so much, but if she said she could do what she promised, it would be worth every damned penny.

Chapter Two – ... And Things Got Worse

Chicago, Illinois

Thursday morning, the Chief of Staff for Mercy General summoned Khloe to his office. Years of working in the medical field as a nurse had gifted her with the perfect poker face which gave away no reaction, whether it was good news she needed to deliver or bad news which had to be explained. Her facial expression did not falter as she sat in front of Dr. Wells listening to him and the head of Human Resources explain why she would be placed on a leave of absence for the situation in the ER.

"Do you understand what we are saying, Ms. Burgess?" Jennifer Conners, head of HR asked.

"I understand it perfectly," Khloe said. "To keep from getting sued by patrons waiting to be seen, it's best that I not be seen."

"Khloe, it's nothing like that," Dr. Wells lied. "In light of the situation, along with a bit of counseling for such a traumatic ordeal, plus the loss of your mother, we are giving you time to get your personal affairs in order."

"My personal affairs are just fine," she said, maintaining the stoic face. "I need to stay busy and work."

"Yes," Jennifer said with that same patronizing tone she used when she fired people. "You may need to work to stay busy, but lives are at stake. A distraction could be deadly to one of our patients."

"Waiting for nearly 24 hours to be seen by a doctor because you don't have enough insurance can also be deadly, but I don't see you changing any of your policies regarding that," Khloe said. "I also don't see you changing any of your policies regarding fraternization and Dr. Lombardi's overprescribing the use of his penis to every female employee."

"Hmm, regarding that," Jennifer said with the barely-there lips pressed together. "We will have to reprimand you for calling his wife and creating such a volatile situation in the ER."

"Bitch, are you high?" Khloe said before she knew it. "I didn't call that woman and God is my witness, I won't even allow Dr, Lombardi to breath on me let alone have intimate relations with the man!"

"If you didn't call Mrs. Lombardi, then who did?" Dr. Wells asked.

Khloe Burgess was many things, but a snitch wasn't on her list. As much as she wanted that crazy ass Vicky out from under her feet, turning her in was not cool. The situation between her and a married man was a job for God.

"Maybe the person who is actually sleeping with him," she said. "I suggest you start there."

"Ms. Burgess, take the leave of absence," Jennifer commented.

"Or what?" Khloe asked. "Are you intending to make my leave permanent when I am gone, whether or not I accept this unwanted help you are offering for my mental recovery?"

Jennifer handed a business card for Employee Services to Khloe, strongly suggesting she take the time. "We shall see you in two weeks," Jennifer said with her shit eating smile.

That was the cue to leave. Standing slowly, she thought hard about cleaning out her locker and never coming back. The second thought which came to her like a hurling pile of bricks was to shoot them all double fisted birds like an angry child on a playground. But she didn't. Their actions would not be dignified with a response as she walked from the offices and out of Mercy General with her back rigid and the stoic face which had become her trademark.

Khloe made her way to the silver Jeep Rubicon that she'd grown to love. It was the only real possession that remained after the bonfire that had consumed her home. Driving to the home that she'd grown up in, she parked her vehicle and sat looking at the structure which felt as nasty on the outside as it was within.

"Feels like my life," Khloe mumbled as she let herself in the three-bedroom home where she'd grown up.

The stench hit her first and against her better judgment, she began to open windows covered in burglary bars, praying fresh air would find its way inside. In a whirlwind of activity, she vacuumed, dusted, sprayed, wiped, mopped, cleaned, and threw out any and everything that smelled. Her phone chimed and she reluctantly stopped to look at the message. It was Joey, who wanted her to call him.

She did.

"Hey Joey," she mumbled.

"Hello, my beautiful Nubian queen, I have great news," he said in the New York accent she used to think was sexy.

"Would it be too much to think you had a change of personality and are bringing back my jewelry?"

He laughed into the line. That skin crawling laugh of a Bond villain right before they began to describe in detail all the ways they planned to kill you. Painfully.

"No doll, I have a plane ticket waiting for you in the morning to come to New York," he said with pride. "It's on Delta. Just check in and join me for the weekend."

"I could use the getaway," she said, not wanting to fill him in on the horrific turn of events in her life.

"Great! I'll send a car for you, then we head down to Atlantic City when this tourney is over and have a good time playing the slots," he said cheerfully.

"I don't gamble, Joey," she reminded him.

"Hey, you took a gamble on me, and look how it's turned out," he said, lying to her with his catchphrase, "Love you, doll."

Joey Montana was a two-bit hustler with a silver tongue and the ability to make a woman orgasm even if he wasn't touching her. Ruefully, she admitted that is why she was with the man. The sex was amazing even if the man was a low-life con artist. At least this way, she didn't have anything left for him to steal.

She sat on the worn couch. Puffs of stink oozed out of the fabric when her butt made contact with the pillow. Disgusted, she began to drag the couch across the living room and out on the street. In this neighborhood, it would be gone before the last rays of sun touched the back of the couch.

It took a bit of effort, but she got the old couch to the curb, followed by the two wing-backed chairs and the smelly old recliner her mother slept in as she half-watched her soap operas. One thing became obvious with the furniture gone. The carpet was woefully gross and disgusting as the furniture which it had rested upon. Clean patches provided a stark contrast to the darkened carpets that used to be beige. Using the anger which rested just below the epidermis of her soul, Khloe located a box cutter to use as a weapon and she began to slice the carpet into manageable sections, hauling it out to the curb as well. In less than an hour, the dirty carpeting was no more and hardwood floors in need of a shitload of TLC stared back at her.

"Well, I have two weeks," she said, taking a seat at the dining room table. The walls of the room were filled with photos of their childhood, pre-walkout of Ricky Burgess. The living room walls, in contrast, were filled with framed photos of the same two children, holding no smiles and sadness in their eyes.

Khloe could almost pinpoint the exact day, in the exact year, in the specific month that she'd stopped being able to smile, the small action requiring very few muscles around her mouth to move in order to create an emotion that others would take as enjoyment or friendliness. She had no friendly left in her. Just anger. Enough anger to work out large chunks of it by a hard ride on Joey before she sent him home.

Anger was the only emotion she truly had left. The men in her life had become a grave disappointment as they all ran from the bottle of poison who was her mother. Deep inside, she knew it was a daughter's duty to grieve the loss of Erica Burgess, but she was glad the bitch was gone. Setting herself and all of Khloe's possessions on fire was a fitting end to a demon who tortured everyone she came in contact with, whether they'd done harm to her or not.

"Dorian," she said aloud, looking at the photo of her older brother. They didn't speak to each other much, if at all. The occasional phone call on birthdays and the required Merry Christmas text had become the norm over the years. Erica had done this to them. Pitting her children against each other during her bouts of sobriety and even worse, during her bouts of fallen down drunkenness. Unlike Dorian, Khloe never reached out to Ricky Burgess. In her estimation, the man was a traitor.

Dorian didn't feel that way and left her alone with Erica when he turned 13 and moved to Indiana with his father. That's how she thought of Ricky Burgess, as Dorian's father. She never considered him to be hers. A father wouldn't abandon his children to be raised by a drunkard with low self-esteem.

Low esteem or not, Erica Burgess went to work five days a week and drank from the end of shift on Friday until the end of the day on Saturday at 11:58 pm. Sunday, she slept all day, rising to urinate and throw meat and beans in a crockpot. The good side, because there was no bright one, was that Erica never brought men home. Their home was secured with burglar bars and an alarm system which was armed from the moment she cracked open the bottle to the last drop to touch her lips on Saturday night. Most Sundays, the house remained locked as well. During the week, she sat with Khloe doing homework, the regular Tuesday visit to the hairdresser, and grocery shopping on Wednesdays. To the outside world, Erica was a hard-working, single, good mom.

In the inside world of the Burgess home, she was a closet drunk. For Khloe, she was a sad woman afraid to face her failures who cowered in glass bottles of expensive booze to force blackouts that prevented a daily dance with reality. During the day, Erica was a Charge Nurse in Obstetrics. The irony of such a sad woman caring for sick children never escaped Khloe since such a sick woman barely cared for her own children.

She looked about the house. "At least it smells better," she said, looking at her phone. "I have to make the call."

Reluctantly she dialed her brother.

"Hey," Dorian said.

"Hey back," Khloe said.

"How is she?" He asked.

"Burned down my house with herself in it," she said solemnly. She waited a few seconds not sure whether to expect a gasp of horror or a sigh of relief. "I'm cremating the rest of what was left. If you want some of the ashes, let me know. If not, I will put her in an urn and keep her in the dining room in china hutch."

"You are so cold, Khloe," Dorian said.

"I am living in the old house because yesterday she burned down mine and everything in it, Dorian. Not sure how you expect me to feel at this moment," she said. "The only pair of drawers I currently own are the ones I'm wearing and the pair in my locker at work."

"Do you need me to do anything? Help you plan a homegoing ceremony or... not really an or situation, in this case," he said. "She is already cremated, so to speak."

"There is no 'or' in this case," Khloe said. "She had no friends. Family stopped coming around years ago, so I will just pick up her ashes."

"Should I come to town, have dinner with you this weekend, say our farewells?" He asked.

"We both said farewell to her years ago, Dorian. This is just the formality of closing out this body," she said. "Stay where you are. I'm heading to New York for the weekend to gather my thoughts."

"Sis," he said with that sorrowful blowing of his breath into the phone. "I'm sorry for your loss."

"Thanks," she said, hanging up.

She too was sorry. The words that hung on her lips she couldn't utter as she fell asleep on the old futon in the guest room. A realization wafted up through the fibers and stuffing, reminding Khloe that her mother had also pissed on this piece of furniture too.

Weariness covered her like a blanket as she lay there, too tired to get up, too broken to care, and too hurt to move. She needed a change. A reason to smile if, in fact, the muscles around her mouth still worked to perform the function of pulling back fleshly lips to expose teeth to sunlight.

The saddest part to Khloe came at three in the morning when hunger woke her, but she was too tired to even eat.

"THE CAUSE OF DEATH was smoke inhalation," the Coroner had pronounced on Erica Burgess, then he asked if he could keep the body.

"Excuse me?" Khloe said.

"I'm so sorry for your loss, but your mother is a rare creature," he said. "True her liver was 60% corroded, but her heart and muscle tone were extraordinary for a woman who drank as she did. Her body would make a great case study."

"Dr. Squibb," she said, "you have known my mother for years. When she worked at this hospital and beyond. To ask me such a thing is bordering on offensive."

"Khloe, you are a fine nurse and good person," Dr. Squibb said. "I have been your counsel and an extra set of ears when you needed one. So please, allow me to advise you on this. Your mother, God rest her sodden soul, took great care of the sick children in the hospital and by the looks of the way you turned out, also took care of you as well. Donating her body will give us and her a chance to continue doing well for others."

"You speak of her with such fondness," she said shocked.

"Let me show you something," he told her, grabbing his wallet. He pulled out a photo of him and a young Erica, who smiled brightly. "This was before...when she actually smiled. You look a lot like her, just wish you smiled more, Khloe."

"This life has given me limes, Dr. Squibb. I can't make lemonade from limes," she said woefully.

"You can make a difference to science, and you won't have to worry about cremation or services, but you can leave her with me to continue doing work in this hospital," Dr. Squibb said.

"Fine," she said, giving herself one less thing to worry about. "Where do I sign?"

"Here," he said, having the paperwork already prepared in a neat little red folder. "I also have the death certificate for you and again, I am sorry for your loss."

"Thank you," she told him, taking the packet of certificates with her to the old house. Her mother had made the last payment on the house two years before she retired. The woman rarely drove, which left the 1999 Buick in the garage almost like new. Erica was never one to believe in making a lot of bills, which left whatever insurance money from the substantial policies to Khloe. Erica left her daughter a rich woman.

Armed with a backpack loaded with the one dress she had left at her mother's, a pair of hose, and heels, she drove the airport to catch her flight to New York. A trip that would change everything in the life of Khloe Burgess.

Chapter Three – … This Sh*t is Hard …

Harbuck, Tennessee

It didn't matter how many times he looked at it, the text he composed ended up being a pile of dog crap. The whole phrasing and sentence structure resonated of a man with an eighth-grade education. He'd earned his degrees in Computer Science from the University of Tennessee. At 42 years old, he prided himself on running a small business that brought in big dollars, not that he had a great number of opportunities to spend any of it. The small business, which employed his brother, three cousins, and a cousin-in-law who had trouble tying his boots, took everybody to provide service to a region of people who didn't trust the government. They trusted him though. A Montgomery name on a satellite dish or a cell phone tower meant the government wasn't listening in on mountain folk business.

Most of the people didn't have much to talk about other than growing crops on the side of a mountain, running shine through the hills, and making hillbilly heroin to sell to a generation that grew dumber by the day. Looking at his words on the computer screen, he felt the same damned way — dumb.

"This shit is hard," he grumbled as he typed three more sentences that were worse than the last four. "I need some help."

He picked up his cell phone and dialed the Courthouse.

"Janet, I need to speak with Jethro," he said to the receptionist. A few minutes later, his cousin came on the line.

"This here's Jethro Montgomery," he said through the phone.

"It's me," Beau said. "I need some help."

"Can you be more specific, please?" Jethro said. "Help moving furniture. Help moving a satellite dish. Help climbing a cell phone tower to change out a blinking light. A man needs to understand what he's consenting to, in plain clear language, before he responds that he is willing to lend a hand."

Exhaling loudly into the phone, Beau almost regretted paying for the online night school law classes for his cousin, but the county needed a Magistrate that the locals trusted. The Montgomery name carried a lot of weight in the area. It was a name that could be trusted. He also trusted Jethro, but he was the one who got Beau into the whole mail order bride thing, and he had 10,000 non-refundable reasons why his cousin should help him.

"I need help writing this ad for my new 'mate,'" he said into a silent phone line. "Hello...Jethro...you there?"

Less than a minute later, his cousin burst through the door. Another drawback to having an office in town was that he was too close to his cousin's workplace.

"Glad you called, let me see what you got there," Jethro said, pushing the bulk of Beau's body to the side. He maneuvered a chair behind the desk while Beau ended the call he was on with the man who now sat behind his desk. "Let me make some magic here."

The keys clicked as Jethro wrote a sentence, deleted it, looked at Beau, scratched his chin, and wrote again. Satisfied with his work, he leaned back in the chair, patted his rounded belly, and flashed his expensive dental work. "Perfecto!" he exclaimed, turning the monitor so Beau could read the 'perfecto' words on the screen.

> *Tennessee Mountain Man seeks a statuesque African American woman with a medical background as a life partner. Applicant must be able to work remotely, be physically fit, and have a love of gardening for cultivating needed food supply. A 4x4 vehicle is also required for travel up and down the painteresque smoky mountains. Childbearing, non-smoker, lover of smoothies, attractive is a plus but not a requirement. A warm and loving lady who enjoys cuddling, board games, and science fiction is sought for a man who likes the same. Ability to cook healthy meals is helpful.*

"That's pretty good, Jethro," Beau said after reading it.

"Great, let's send this puppy to the Mail Order Bride lady and see if anyone wants to pet it," Jethro said with a huge grin.

"Some days I seriously worry about you," Beau replied.

"Worry all you want, but we need to create you an email account separate from your regular one," Jethro said.

"I've already done all of that," Beau told him. "Coraline has it on file. I just need to email this to her and wait for a statuesque African American woman to follow the trail of breadcrumbs."

"Yeah, to your mountain lair of love," Jethro said waggling his red eyebrows.

"I really don't like you sometimes," Beau said.

"Don't care, long as you love me," Jethro said, making kissy faces at him. "I'm hungry. Jolene made stew today at the café. Lunch is on you, so let's go."

"How did I end up footing the bill for your lunch?"

"Because you called me over here to play Cyrano to your Lady Bear," he said grinning. "Feed me, Signore de Bergerac."

"If that ad works, I will let you marry us," Beau said jokingly.

Beau's mother, Honey Sherman Montgomery, needed to made aware of what he'd just done. God was forgiving; Honey Montgomery, not so much. After work, he would make the drive up the mountain and have supper with his folks. It could be months before he got a bite on the ad, or even a year, the lady told him, but he paid his money, so he would wait.

Good things came to those who waited. At least that's what his folks taught him. This would be a testament to their teachings or a hard life lesson to swallow.

THE BLACK TOWN CAR waited for Khloe on the curb in front of the airport. A driver, a tall, slim, Black man in dark shades, held a hand-written sign with her misspelled name. She was unable to control the case of irritation that had traveled on the plane with her as she sat in the cheap seats sandwiched between a fat man with gas and a sweaty lady with sinus issues.

"I'm Koe Bungness," she said facetiously.

"Right this way," the man said, opening the back door. "Do you have any luggage?"

"No, I travel light," she said, getting into the back seat. There was nothing to say to the man, and against her better judgment, she napped quietly as they sat in traffic, headed into midtown to the Baccarat Hotel.

"Mr. Montana will be waiting for you in the bar," the driver said. Tipping the driver a twenty, she thanked him and made her way inside.

Knowing Joey as she did, he won big last night and splurged on the $500 a night hotel suite. That was his way. Hot and cold and prone to impulses, which as a couple, made them more opposite than seemed attractive. In the Army, his government name was Joseph Greenwood. To the poker circuit, he was known as Joey Montana. The idiot had never been to Montana and when asked, he truly believed the state sat below Utah. He was good looking and great in bed. A girl can overlook stupid for those two reasons alone.

"Look at you, all tall, dark, and gorgeous. Where's your luggage?" Joey asked.

"Long story short, my Mom got drunk and burned down my house," she said flatly, raising her hand for the bartender to bring her whatever was handy. The guy in the crisp white shirt behind the bar held up a bottle of red wine. Khloe used her thumbs to indicate he needed to go higher. The bartender held up a brandy and a gin. She opted for the brandy.

"At least she saved you a nice dress. I like the one you're wearing," he said with that charming *I'm going to get me some of that* smile. "Love those heels as well. They make your legs look like they go on for days."

"Joey, I lost my house and my mother, and you want to talk to me about my dress?"

"Oh wow, Erica is gone?"

"Yes, she died of smoke inhalation," she said.

"I'm sorry to hear that. Baby, are you okay?"

"Not really. I lost my mother," Khloe said to him. "My house is a pile of ashes and my job put me on administrative leave for two weeks after crazy Vicky called Lombardi's wife and used my name, and the woman came to the hospital and shot up the place. It's been a bitch of a week."

The bartender arrived with a glass of brandy that she downed in one swallow. The expression on Joey's face read like an old movie where you knew the plot twist before it was halfway over. *More bad news. Why bring me way to New York to give me bad news? He could have told me this shit over the phone.*

"Spit it out, Joey – life's too short to pull your punches and save your aces," she said, waiting for him.

He held his hands folded into each other. The thick thumb, which often brought her pleasure and eased the tension in her shoulders, rubbed over his fingers as he tried to find the courage he never possessed. She had the poker face the man craved but also never possessed. A sad trait for a man who played the game for a living.

"I have great news, my Nubian love," he said, running his fingers over the thin mustache that made him look like the maintenance man in a bad porno flick.

Joey, tall and slim with just enough muscles for a girl to hold on to, had warm, cocoa butter skin, dark brown eyes, and jet-black hair. On a good day, the man reminded her of a Latin lover, even though he was born and bred on the south side of Chicago to a family of hustlers. He had 12 years of service in the Army but was chaptered out for selling food and goods to the Afghanis, which always made her question his scruples. Hell, the man would give her jewelry and take it back to play a poker game. Scruples weren't the reason she semi-dated him.

"Let me hear it," she said, raising her hand for another drink.

She sipped as Joey went over the details of the new contract he signed with a traveling poker show that got televised on a network no one watched. Joey spoke softly as he told her that he was leaving in the morning. His shifty eyes darted back and forth while the explanation of how they could no longer see each other rolled off his lips. Once more he offered his condolences on the loss of her mother. He apologized for the loss of her entire life, then handed her an expensive bracelet to replace the jewelry he'd taken.

"Are you breaking up with me?" Khloe asked in disbelief.

"Not breaking up, per se, but I'm going to be gone all the time. You know city to city," he said.

"Like you are now," she said with no emotion in her voice.

"But baby...you have to understand, I don't want to be unfaithful, and I'm going to be balling," he said.

Khloe's eyebrows arched incrementally as she found her words. Hateful words eked up first but she tamped them down. Spiteful words filled her mouth but those she swallowed. Instead, the smile she often tried to form on her lips only resulted in a downward scowl as she found her voice.

"So, tonight was to be a farewell fuck and wish me well?" she asked.

"Well, when you put it like that...I mean, dinner, the bracelet, wish me well when I pack up in the morning, rub the junk for good luck kind of thing," he said.

"I can't stand you," she said, standing on shaky legs. The liquor hit her empty stomach and was making everything fuzzy. "Only you would book a night in a hotel named after gambling. Your punk ass flew me all the way to New York for a final fuck and to wish you well. I hope you lose your shirt, ass, and the rest of your self-respect."

She tried to maintain hers as she slung the backpack over her shoulder and left through the glass double doors. Common sense would have told Khloe to head towards the counter and book herself a room, but she had a point to make. Tonight, she was walking out of his life and her ass would be the last thing he saw.

Halfway down the sidewalk, she realized she was drunk. An unfriendly man saw she was as well and snatched the backpack off her shoulder and took off running. Without hesitation, she kicked off the heels and took off after him, catching him by the back of his jacket, yanking hard, bring him down flat on his back. She climbed on top of his chest, pressing his arms down with her knees and pummeling his face with her small balled up fists. The assailant screamed like a three-year-old girl, bucking underneath Khloe as he thrashed on the sidewalk, tossing her off his chest.

"Crazy lady!" he screamed as he ran away.

Khloe sat on the sidewalk, gripping her backpack, her feet bleeding from running three city blocks barefooted. The tears she refused to shed demanded acknowledgment of their presence. The pain which poked her in the chest asked for an audience as well. The culmination of loss, loneliness, and failure to be anything in this life other than a nurse or a nursemaid to selfish people who commanded she serve slapped her hard across the face.

The tears began to roll down her cheeks and a loud wail came from the recesses of her soul and she howled. She howled for the loss of the sorriest a mother a girl could ever have who had left this earth without even having an opportunity to be better or say farewell. She groaned as she balled into a small fetus position on a filthy sidewalk in New York City, upset with a father she didn't know who had set the precedent of her understanding of relationships with men. It resonated to her core because she always picked the worst losers on the planet to try and build a life. A life that was now devoid of any heft. A life that had taken the fight right out of her soul.

"Come on, baby, get up off the ground," the voice said. "This is no place for a lady to break down."

The gentle hands were soft. The voice soothing to the weary soul as Khloe was helped to her feet. The tears blurred her eyes as she blindly followed a person she couldn't see who may have been leading her to the car where she would be put into a sex trafficking ring. At least then, she would feel something.

"My name is Coraline, and I'm going to clean up those feet and get a cup of tea in you and some food," the nice lady said. "Come on now, in my office. Let me take care of you."

"I try to be a good person, but this shit is hard," Khloe said, feeling lightheaded. She saw the settee and reached for it. Her body barely made the connection before all went dark.

Chapter Four – ... My Name is Khloe Burgess

N*ew York City, Avenue of the Americas*

Shades of gray materialized as Khloe tried to open her eyes. A dull pain thudded on the left side of her head as she tried to sit upright, but she gave up and lay back on the cushions of the flower covered chaise lounge. With her eyes closed, she could smell the faint aroma of lavender and vanilla which calmed her a bit, but she needed to get up, find a place to stay for the night, and eat. Maybe the lightheadedness, she surmised, was from lack of eating.

"Oh good, you are awake," Coraline said as she surveyed the woman. By the look of her clothing, the backpack she carried, and the status of her nails, she was not homeless or a woman on the take. The sadness which hovered around her spirit read as deep hurt insulted by a near robbery.

Khloe's eyelids fluttered as her vision cleared, allowing her to take in the room where her rescuer had given her refuge. The walls were covered in a soft flowered paper that matched the chaise lounge she rested upon. Gentle hands cleaned the open cuts and pulled away damaged the skin on her feet. The decorative hose with the intricate designs was ruined and the mangled toe covering rested on the floor, splattered with speckles of blood. The $30 pair of sexy leg coverings now resembled a pair of leggings.

"Thank you," Khloe mumbled as she came to a sitting position.

"Hold still, I need to make sure there is no dirt or debris in those cuts and get this salve on your feet and some bandaging. I looked for your shoes but honestly, I had no idea which direction you ran from," she told Khloe. "Looks like you had a rough day."

"Lady, it has been a rough month," she mumbled, pulling her feet away. "I can do that – you don't have to."

"Seems to me as if you could use someone to take care of you for a change," Coraline said. "Women these days have forgotten what it feels like to be taken care of - always arguing they don't need anyone to take care of them and that they can take care of themselves. While I admire the sentiment and the meaning behind it, at the end of the day, we all want to matter to someone. Do you matter to anyone?"

"Right now, no. I'm not even sure I matter to myself," she said forlornly.

"May I inquire as to what happened to you?"

Khloe's vision cleared as she gazed at the walls covered in photos of old white women, ladies in prairie dresses standing next to wagon trains with sober expressions at the idea of heading west. Each wall had images of decades of women in varying dresses for the respective era, standing beside a young woman with a bobbed haircut and intense eyes. The ladies in the images looked like an exact replica of the one cleaning her feet.

"Are these your relatives?" Khloe asked, ignoring the statements.

"Yes, nearly six generations of matchmakers, since the first wagon trains went west in 1843," Coraline said with pride. "You are diverting my question about what happened to you."

"I'm not diverting," Khloe replied. "I'm just not in the business of telling my woes to complete strangers."

"My name is Coraline Newair. I'm a Scorpio and professional expert in the ways of love. I also love tea and lemon biscuits with a drizzle of clover honey. Let's see, I'm allergic to bullshit, dumb men, and polyester," she said. "Now we are no longer strangers. Your turn."

"I'm Khloe Burgess, a Nurse Practitioner from Chicago. A former soldier in the Army Corps of Nurses and retired after 20 years. I have horrible taste in men and lived with a functioning alcoholic as a mother, who earlier this week burned down my house with herself in it," Khloe said.

"Good gravy," Coraline said, touching her arm. "You are grieving the loss of your mother and nearly got mugged to boot. Did you come to New York for a moment of solace?"

"No, I came to meet my boyfriend who is a professional child who fancies himself to be a poker player. He is terrible at the game and even worse at life. I can read his tells so easily and saw through this latest scheme of his," Khloe said.

"Scheme?"

"Yeah, he flew me to New York to break up with me, but of course, he planned to do it on the way out of the hotel door in the morning," she said, looking about for her belongings. "I need to get going and find somewhere to stay tonight. Can you recommend a hotel, close by, considering the shoes in my bag aren't made for walking?"

"No, tonight you are going to keep me company," Coraline said. "I can use some and you could use a friend. We will order in some dinner, settle in for the night with a nice glass of Bordeaux, and turn on the television while it watches us."

Khloe's bottom lip quivered as the tears welled in her eyes. It had been so long since a person did a nice thing for her without wanting payment in return. Or did she?

"What is it going to cost me?"

"In my world, women don't pay a dime, so it shall cost you nothing. Hopefully, by the end of the weekend, you will leave with some answers and a new direction in your life," Coraline said.

"From your mouth to God's ears, but why are you doing this for me?"

"Because we all need a friend, and sister, you look like you could really use an ear, a few hugs and a good night's rest," Coraline said. "Come on, I am closing up. I live upstairs."

"Thank you for all of this," Khloe said, looking at the perfectly bandaged feet. "I really don't want to impose upon you any more than I have."

"Oh pshaw! It beats eating alone and talking to the imaginary cat that people assume I have," Coraline said, moving to the front office and securing the door. She led the way to the back elevator after turning down the lights, leaving a soft pink glow about the room. Khloe didn't know why, but she felt safe with her new friend.

"Lead on," Khloe said, trying to walk and not damage the fresh bandages.

THE APARTMENT WAS EXACTLY what Khloe expected. A whole lot of New York with no personal style to the place. The fridge was empty, the wine rack full, and loads of expensive paintings hanging from the wall reminding all who entered the space that the lady came from old money. A quick trip to the ladies' room and Khloe returned to find the table set with dishes and hot food ready for consumption.

"I played it safe and ordered chicken," Coraline said. "Everybody eats chicken."

"Yeah, that works," Khloe said, taking a seat. "Coraline, do you mind me asking what it is you do for a living? You said a professional love ...something or other?"

"My family has run a mail order bride service since 1843. My mother ran the company before me, and her mother before her and my daughter shall inherit the company as soon as I find the right man to be my life mate," she said.

"Lifemate?"

"Yes, most people don't understand the concept of marriage," Coraline said. "In my many years of experience, I have turned away quite a few women applicants that are enamored with the idea of the white dress and getting gifts, planning for the wedding and not the relationship."

"I assume since your family has been doing this for so long that business is good," she said.

"There are times when it hasn't been, but out there in the real America are men who want to be married to women who want to be married to them," she said. "We have a 99% success rate."

"And the 1% of failures?"

"Well," Coraline said, plating the chicken and pouring the wine. A couple of quick glass clicks to toast the meal and she sipped, swallowed, and gathered her thoughts. "Every now and then we get a woman who signs up, gets to the location, and says, 'Oh, hell no.' It's rare but it does happen. Then last year, I had an incident which shook all of us to the core. A mail-order bride went missing."

"What?" Khloe asked.

"Down in the Georgia mountains. She was set to marry one man, who sent his brother to pick her up, and the brother absconded with her," Coraline said. "Kept that poor woman in a cabin in the woods for nearly a year. But she escaped and found help and delivered her baby on another man's floor."

"This is juicy," Khloe said. "The chicken is as well, but this story. Please go on."

"Khloe, it gets better. The man married her and kept that child as his own," Coraline said with the corners of her lips forming a smile. "The really cute part is that her friends came looking for me to give me, you know, the once over.

Ironically, the man's brothers, the Neary Brothers as I call them, showed up to stop the two friends from opening a can of trouble."

Khloe chewed anxiously, swallowing and shoveling more food in her mouth as she listened intently.

"I set the four of them up as couples, of course, added a bit of romantic magic, and his brothers are married to his wife's best friends," she said with a smile. "The youngest brother, Isiah, he and DeShondra just got married. Little did they know I was in the back of the church. Lovely couple. Good life mates."

"You make it seem so easy," Khloe said. "Finding a life mate is hard in this world where everyone wants to swipe a butt and move on the next one. I don't even want to talk about kids and a warm home that doesn't revolve around the internet and fancy cars. To me, at this point in my life, I just want simple. I could care less for a TV at this point."

"Khloe, will you let me help you?"

"Help me do what? Become a mail order bride and run the risk of being kept in a cabin by a man with three teeth as his love monkey? I'm with that one chick, oh hell no," Khloe said with a straight face.

"Again, she and the other were an anomaly in thousands of matches," Coraline said. "Answer me this, what is it you want out of a relationship?"

"I want to love a man who takes care of himself. Meat at every meal means you are going to die," she said. "I want kids but I am pushing 40, which means I have to spit a few out real fast, or I will be sitting in the audience at my kids' high school graduations and people will think I'm their Grandma."

"You still haven't told me what it is you want in a relationship, Khloe. You said kids and a man who takes care of himself, but you can't build a relationship off of that," she told her.

Khloe thought long and hard about her last four relationships. The things that had gone wrong and the things that had been right. Smushing them all together, she gave a well-thought-out answer.

"I want a man who loves to cuddle, not just the sex portion. A man who wants to know me and what makes me tick. I love my smoothies in the morning, fresh air, and a garden tended with care. Even though I don't watch a great deal of television, I really enjoy *Game of Thrones* and discussing a good book after dinner over a glass of brandy seated next to a man who pushes me to be better," Khloe said. "More importantly, I want to be in a relationship with a man who wants to be committed to being in a relationship with me. Coraline, I want to be loved and adored. Thoughtful gifts made by hand versus a shiny trinket found in a window. Does that make sense?"

"More than you know," Coraline said. "Would you believe me if I told you that man walked into my office downstairs this past Monday?"

"No," Khloe replied.

"Well he did," she said. "However, I can't just put the two of you together. There are a series of test, health screenings, personality profiles, and the like."

"Tomorrow is Saturday, and unless you have plans, I am ready to get started," she said. "To think the man, I just described is out there and waiting for me, I feel anxious."

"No, my love, for the first time in a long time, you are feeling hopeful," she said. "I say we do it right after dinner."

Most of the night passed with Coraline and Khloe huddled up taking Khloe through a battery of tests. She had blood drawn and was told she needed to give a poop sample. At the end of the night, with her information plugged into the Perfect Match database, Khloe Burgess was perfectly matched with five men.

"The one in Hawaii sounds promising," Coraline said.

"Yeah, but it's an island. There is no way off an island other than boat or plane," Khloe said. "In case of inclement weather, neither of those are an option to escape danger."

"Arizona?"

"Too hot and no grass or greenery," she said. "I can't grow a garden in the desert, and the amount of water it would take to yield a decent crop would be scandalous."

"New Hampshire, Vermont...the husband to be in Vermont is pretty sexy, and he owns an apple orchard," Coraline said.

"Too cold in the winter," she said. "I live in Chicago. It would be nice to spend a winter and not freeze my ass off."

"Tennessee it is," Coraline said, pressing the key to bring up the photo of Beauregard Sherman Montgomery.

"Whoa, he looks like the leader of the Aryan Knighthood," Khloe said. She leaned forward towards the screen staring into the eyes. "This man likes to cuddle and drink smoothies?"

"Yes," Coraline said. "He was also the one who walked into my office on Monday. I think he came just in time to set the stage to meet you."

Khloe turned around to look at Coraline. Words hung between them as her eyes went back to the screen to her potential new husband. A man who enjoyed watching *Game of Thrones* and drinking smoothies and had a nice garden just off the back porch. The picture Coraline pulled up showed it.

"I'm not sure what to say here, Coraline," she said.

"Thanks, would be helpful," the matchmaker replied.

"Normally, I wait for the test results to come back, but this one, I have a good feeling about," she said. "Here is his e-mail. Reach out, start a dialogue and see where it leads. I'm going to bed."

"Goodnight," Khloe said as she stared at Beau, as he liked to be called. He was a lot of man. Six feet four, over two hundred pounds, the sides of his hair shaven and his arms covered in tattoos. "He could keep me warm in winter."

In the guest room which held even less personality than the rest of the apartment, Khloe sat on the side of the bed and read again his ad for a life mate. *Reach out, start a dialogue.* Pulling her laptop from the bag she'd fought like a hellcat to keep and pressing the start button, she waited for the little apple to show up. Logging into her off the books e-mail account, she sent a message, nice and simple.

July 28, 2018

"Dear Beau,

My name is Khloe Burgess. I am responding to your ad for a life mate. I meet all the criteria of what you need, but I think it's only fair to tell you I am responding to the ad in hopes you can provide a bit of reciprocity.

I answered the ad in optimism that you can help me find my smile again.

Looking forward to your response.

Chilled out in Chi-Town

Chapter Five – … My Dearest Khloe

H*ooters Holler, Kentucky*

Beauregard drove through the back roads and gulleys into the area of the Smoky Mountains few people dared enter, Hooters Holler. The small valley, nestled inside of some of the prettiest countryside God ever created, had been inhabited by generations of Montgomery's since the Civil War. Others had moved into the area as well, creating a close-knit community of patriots who lived off the land and cared for their neighbors.

The only problem was that many had never left the Holler nor did they plan to do so in the near future, but Beau had. He left to attend summer camps and to attend college and understand the outside world to return and teach those in Hooter's Holler about the changes going on around them. The best way, he figured, to teach and show the people is to let them see it for themselves. At the University of Tennessee, he majored in Computer Science, coming back to the Holler and setting up an affordable cable company to offer his neighbor's satellite television and cell phones. No more runners with messages to the neighbors, but actual cell phones.

It wasn't an easy sell. Many in the Holler still believed the government was spying on them and the radiation from the cell towers would turn them into blathering automatons for the 'C.I. of A'. However, the Montgomery name was attached to the company, which meant the folks could trust Beau since he was all educated and understood the new world of race mixing and dancing suggestively in public. For folks in the Holler, those types of things were reserved for the wedding night and special occasions like baby-making nights.

He practiced several times what he would, in fact, say about his latest decision to take an unconventional approach to marriage to very conventional mountain folk parents. Albus, his father, knew his eldest son was a bit different, and he'd made concessions and even worked outside of the Holler to make money to send the boy to computer camps and to college. Albus understood

Beau. His mother Honey thought the sun rose and set on the boy's every choice and seldom if ever questioned his decision making. Beau only hoped that today would be the same.

"Hey Pa," he said, parking his truck. He left the office early today to come for supper in the hills, hoping his Ma was making his favorite, possum stew.

"Son," Albus said, taking a puff or three off his corn cob pipe. The old blue eyes looked grayer these days as cataracts began to take over. The weathered skin of too many days in the sun had taken effect, and his father fit the stereotype of an old mountain man with a few good teeth remaining in his head. Albus was a good father and Beau had no complaints.

"Albus, is that Beau I hear out there?" Honey Montgomery called from inside. The beautiful, shoulder length honey blond hair which had begun to gray over the years still shone like the sun was following behind her head as she walked.

"It's me, Ma," he said, handing her bags of flour and sugar, along with a box of fancy chocolates he'd picked up in New York.

"I hear tell you went up to New York City," Honey said looking at the box of chocolatey delights.

"Yes'm," he replied, looking down at the toe of his boots.

"Oh, possum nuts in a squirrel's mouth," Albus said. "We know that look, Honey. That's the same dumb ass looks he gives us when he's done gone and dun sumpin' stupid."

"Lordy be, Beau, who's pregnant?" Honey asked.

"No one is pregnant," Beau said, snapping his head up to look at his parents' eye to eye.

"Well, what is it, boy?" Albus demanded.

Beauregard feared no man and very few beasts, however, he did fear having to tell his parents what he'd done on a whim. The logic behind his decision was sound. His happiness was at stake and he deserved some of that in a royal flush. Inhaling deeply, he rattled off his decision.

"Ma, Pa, I'm getting married," he said.

"To who? Ain't that many eligible girls left in these Hollers which would suit you," Albus said. "You're bringing in an outsider?"

"Pa, I think we have to at this point. The last County doctor left two years ago and we haven't even been able to even get a nurse in these parts. We are just too country poor to sustain one," Beau said.

"How does this impact the stupid thing you did?" Albus asked.

"What makes you think I did a stupid thing?"

"The way you're shuffling your weight from foot to foot," Albus said. "Spit it out before I die of a brain fart trying to figure you out."

"I placed an ad for a mail-order bride," Beau said in a whoosh of air.

Albus leaned forward in the creaky old rocker that his father, Joe Boy, had handcrafted from a fallen tree. His left eye half closed as a circle of smoke rose up from the pipe, getting into his eye and making it water. One-eyed, he looked at his son then his wife.

"You like to do that freaky stuff in bed with things that require batteries and Vaseline don't you?" Albus asked.

"Pa!" Beauregard said. "No, that's not why I did it. I placed an ad for a woman who likes the things I like and has a medical background. Times are changing and we need healthcare in whatever form we can get it. You two aren't getting any younger, and I would feel better if my wife had the capabilities to help me take care of you in your later years."

Honey stepped forward. The worn-out apron around her waist had seen better days, but she refused to get rid of it. The plain cotton dress she wore also had lasted longer than the fabric should have, along with the run over shoes she wore that still had tread on the bottom. Beau wanted a savvy wife that would get his mother into a decent pair of shoes and dresses that didn't bear more patches than fabric. He didn't know about those kinds of things, and even when he'd brought her bolts of material, Honey wasn't a seamstress.

"She's a black gal, ain't she?" Honey asked.

"Ma, how do you figure that?"

"Our women ain't never interested you. No matter how many bees flitter around you son, them plain Janes have all bored you to death," Honey said. "I remember that summer at the beach, you found those little Black kids and we didn't see you until suppertime if then. I know you dated one in college. That one we met."

"Would it be so terrible if I did, Ma?" he questioned her, but his eyes were on his father.

"Don't know how well she'll be received in these parts. It will be a challenge," Albus said.

"She will be a Montgomery," Beau said. "It's a name you can trust."

"A medical professional, eh?"

"That what I asked for in my ad," he told his father.

"But why you do have to get a mail order one? Can't you just go to the city and find one in a bar or one of them churches where they do all that fancy singing?" Honey asked. "I saw it them one Sunday morning on the telly."

"I'm not that simple, Ma. I need a woman who gets me and our way of life. She will have to know how to garden and be in good shape, and she may have to help me out from time to time with the business," he said. "I'm not going to find that in some random bar. This way is smarter."

"You are many things, Beau, smart being at the top of the list," Honey said. "But what if she's ugly? No Grandma wants ugly grandbabies."

"I'm not marrying anyone for her looks," he told his parents. "What I want is to find a woman that will not make me want to drive her to the nearest bus station and leave her there. Call me silly, but I want what you two have."

"They broke the mold when they made my Honey," Albus bragged, reaching for his wife of 45 years. "I hear ya, boy, just hope it works out."

"Beau, you know your heart, do what you think is best," she said. "She gone' be from New York?"

"Don't know, Ma. The way this company works she can be from anywhere," he said.

"This sure is exciting," Honey said. "I am going to be the talk of Holler and this side of the mountain. Me with an African American daughter-in-law, or do they like to be called Black? I know the term Negro is no longer used."

"Black is fine, Ma," he said, giving a small smile.

"Hmmpff," Albus said, changing the subject to his rumbling belly. "I'm hungry, them vittles ready, woman?"

"Don't you woman me, Albus Montgomery, or you will be eating your supper out of that dog bowl there," Honey said to her husband.

"And don't you sass me, woman, in front of the boy. You make me look weak," Albus said.

"Weak is the last thing your children will ever think of you," she said with a flirty smile.

Beauregard watched the interaction between them and his heart skipped a beat. After 45 years they still liked each other, which said a lot. There were very few women he liked after sharing a meal with them, let alone a bed. His dating luck had given way under the pressure of establishing his business, and now that the company ran smoothly, he wanted his home life to as well.

"How long before you know, boy?" Albus asked.

"Know what, Pa?"

"If you have a fish on the line?"

This he wasn't sure about at all. It could be a month, a year, or in the next 15 minutes, but he didn't want to tell them that. As if the gods had heard the unspoken pleas in his heart, his phone buzzed. Looking at the screen, the green notification showed he'd received a new email in the account he set up for the mail-order bride. His brow furrowed as he opened the message and read the words.

He smiled.

Honey smiled, too.

Albus waited for an answer, but seeing the smile on his son's face, he knew the fish were biting. The idea made the old man give a gapped tooth grin as well.

"Can't wait to meet her," Albus said.

"Ooh, this is so exciting. Do you have a photo?" Honey asked.

Beau scrolled through the message, coming to the bottom and clicking on the attachment. A face popped up, covering the screen of the phone. He froze. His hand went to his chest as he looked at the ebony beauty staring back at him. Slowly he turned the phone around to show his parents.

"Is that the first choice or do ya get to pick from the litter?" Albus asked. "She's kind of scrawny. Seems like you wouldn't want the last Christmas tree on the lot Charlie Brown."

To Beauregard Montgomery, the little lady was absolutely lovely. He envisioned himself coming home in the evening from work with her waiting for him to discuss the busy day she'd had or the people she helped as they dined over a hearty bowl of stew before settling in for the night. This Khloe may have been the first response, but in his heart, she needed to be the only one.

A sadness in her eyes spoke to the weary soul inside of him that begged to teach the little woman what real love felt like and to give her reason to smile again. He would give her a million reasons each day to curve those sensual lips. Beau took it as a personal challenge. One he planned to make good on.

Supper with his parents became a lesson in active listening since his mind wandered back and forth to the lady. The dark-skinned, thin woman with sad eyes who wanted to smile. Scenario after scenario played out as he mentally re-arranged the house to accommodate her nice dishes, delicately trimmed hand towels, and book collections of Stephen King and Octavia Butler. He really wanted her to have an Octavia Butler collection. *That would be so cool.*

"Go home, Beau, you are no company to us," Honey said. "We might as well have your sister here taking *shelfies* of herself."

"Selfies, Ma," he gently corrected.

"You kids and your fancy new language," his mother replied. "In my day, we had a can with a string through it. My brother would hide behind a tree and we would squirrel hunt via our walkies."

"I'm certain that was a lot of fun," he mumbled as he considered adding a larger mirror to the bathroom. The one he had served for shaving, not clearing your pores of impurities and yanking tiny hairs out of a woman's chin. "Rugs, I need to get some rugs."

"Go home, Beau, and let us know how this turns out," Albus said. "I want some time alone with your Ma."

"You have been alone with her all day," Beau argued.

"No, she was doing her woman's work about the house. I was doing my man's work, you know, hunting, gathering, being strong," Albus said. "The day is done. Time for a man and a woman to settle in for the night. Go home, boy."

"Yes sir," Beau said, writing a response letter in his head to the lovely Khloe woman. He waved farewell to his father, hugged his mother and climbed into the truck. On the drive down the mountain, he rode in silence, going over sweet words in his head to respond to her letter of interest.

By the time he reached the hunting high house, Beau had found the words. Moving quickly, he sat down at the computer, booted up the system, and opened the e-mail to compose his first response to the lady.

July 29, 2018

"Dear Khloe Burgess,

It is a pleasure to ~~meethear from you.~~

WRITING HER BACK BECAME tougher than writing the ad, but he wasn't going to call Jethro over to fill in the spaces for him. All he needed...*this simply required...say what's in your heart, Beau. Establish a friendship, paint a picture of her life with you. Think of the million ways you want to make her smile. Try it again.*

It took two days, loads of scrap paper until he finally found the right words. He sat and composed the response, hoping the lady wouldn't think he was playing games with the delayed reply time.

July 31, 2018

"Dearest Khloe,

From my front porch, the sun crests over the Great Smoky Mountains, breaking that famous layer of white haze which lingers in the trees. A hot cup of black coffee and a good biscuit with a smattering of my Ma's home-made jam will make a soul wonder how the rest of the world lives.

My life is simple. My home is as well.

Optimism is a good friend as I hope you and I will become as well. It is the simpler things in life which make me smile. Hopefully, I can share them with you.

The Tennessee Mountain Man

IT WASN'T MUCH, BUT it would serve as a start. Beau double checked the content, ran the spell checker, and hit reply. He needed to be off to work. The installation in the new schoolhouse started today and half his team would be on the other side of the mountain setting up a new satellite dish. Jethro was right. As clumsy as his team was, the County did need a medical professional.

In his next correspondence with Khloe Burgess, he would find out her medical background. Meanwhile, he had computers to install, a network to create, and a school with loads of technology for the kids in the region opening in a little over a month. He set to work.

KHLOE SAT IN THE OLD house looking about at all the materials, collections, and items Erica had gathered over the years. Their entire lives were in this home. She would be happy to leave it all to the drug dealers and crows; however, small details required her delicate handling, beginning with the farewell to her mother.

Dr. Squibb, the Coroner, left a message for her that Erica's body had been accepted into the program for scientific study at the University. She should have felt alone, but instead, she felt relief coupled with a tinge of excitement. Beauregard Montgomery started the dialogue with a painted picture in words of the home that, if she accepted, they would share. Her heart danced a bit at the offer to become her friend first before sending a dick pic and him with a 'hey girl' smile.

The optimism ran high as she responded back to him.

August 2, 2018

"Dear Beau,

That's a description of a sunrise I'd love to see. The sheer idea of sitting on that front porch at sunset with a nice cup of tea as I read the next chapter in Masello's Einstein Prophecy sounds amazing. As a lover of science fiction, I am anxious to learn what you are reading as well.

In the interest of honesty, I am not broken or running from a life which let me down. The past few months have been intense and I'm seeking a change, one that involves a family and a man who desires to be in a relationship wholeheartedly.

Not sure what all I need to say, but I'm interested in being your life mate.

Chillin' in Chi-Town

BEAU SAT BEHIND HIS desk staring at the monitor. He wanted to say so much, yet writing his feelings wasn't his way. The conversations that should come next required a person-to-person interaction not carefully crafted hidden sentences that said nothing.

Jethro walked into his office with two of Jolene's banana nut muffins and two cups of coffee. The last thing he wanted or needed to hear this morning was his crazy cousin's convoluted conclusions. Not that it mattered. Jethro was going to give it anyway.

"Hey, Beau, any bites on your bear meat?"

"My what?"

"You know, the ad, a lady bear to hibernate with you during the cold winter," he asked. "I think my ad said it all."

Against his better judgment, Beau took out his phone and showed the photo of one Khloe Burgess. Jethro stared at the photo, his head cocked to the side like the RCA dog trying to hear the low-frequency whistle of his master's call. Beau knew that look. The man was going to either make a prolific statement or say something incredibly stupid. He placed his bets on the latter.

"She's cute, but kind of scrawny," Jethro said. "How many others can you chose from or are you going to go with the runt of the litter?"

"Jethro, I am not at the pound choosing a new pet," Beau said, getting to his feet. "This is a human being with dreams, desires, and hopes for a future and a family."

"Okay, so what's the holdup?"

"Whaddya mean?"

"If you think she's the one when is she moving here, because I need to set the wedding date on my calendar to marry you," he said, peering over the rim of the coffee cup. "Remember, you said if it worked out based on my ad, I was going to marry you."

"I hate you often and frequently have throughout the course of our lives," Beau told him.

"Yeah. Yeah. Get her on the phone, set a date, and get her down here before it starts to get cold. You gotta harvest and can the rest of them veggies, and the school's gotta get finished before it opens after Labor Day. Ain't no time for flowery words. You placed the ad, she responded, get her here so we can get ready for winter," Jethro told him.

"You're an ass," Beau said. "But even an ass smells good every now and then."

"I'm just right and you just hate it," he told his cousin. "Get on the phone, get her moved in, and start making some babies."

That wasn't what he wanted. Beauregard Montgomery knew he could get that any local woman in the area. He had asked for a mate. A partner in life. Maybe it was time he explained it better to his Khloe. *My Khloe. I like that.*

August 5, 2018

"My Dear Khloe,

To an extent, we are all broken, drifting aimlessly through the cosmos seeking out another soul to connect and make us whole. In that regard, I guess I too am broken.

This man was broken enough to place an ad and pay money so the cosmos could align for me to find you, or rather, we find each other. At this point, I want to make perfectly clear my intentions and what is expected of the woman who agrees to be my life partner. I have carefully chosen the word life mate because I do not need a wife.

A wife I could acquire locally. To me, there is a distinction between a wife and a life mate. A wife, in my head, cooks, cleans and is pliable when I am on the ready. I am perfectly capable of washing my own clothes, matching my own socks and cooking my meals. What I seek is a woman who is a nurse, a former EMT, or a doctor. Assuming you are one of the three, our County has been without a medical professional for nearly two years. Although the local people here aren't very trusting,

I am confident the woman who is my wife will be allowed to tend to them. She will be a Montgomery – that is a name you can trust.

In the Town of Harbuck, there is a small office which will serve as your workspace. Set your own hours, two or three days a week, and the remaining time is yours. We can spend it together when I am not working. I enjoy hiking, exploring, or traveling as my schedule permits. It would be an honor to share these simple life pleasures with you.

On a different note, Einstein Prophecy's is full of historical inaccuracies. I am reading Mind's Eye, a Nick Hall Book by Douglas E. Richards. Halfway through. Somewhat amused especially with the Russian mafia aspect which could have been left out, but we can discuss both over coffee and my Ma's biscuits.

I am saying that to say this: If you are in and ready to be my life mate, let's stop the correspondence and begin planning to get you here before the first rains in September and the kids go back to school. Plus, them little boogers need shots.

Here is my number – (423-555-4666).

I look forward to hearing your voice.

Your Tennessee Mountain Man

Chapter Six – Tennessee Here I Come...Wait, What?

Chicago, Illinois

The message glared on the screen at Khloe like a fairy tale coming to life. *He wants me to come now. Marry him and start a life. What in the hell?*

Yet the thought of getting the hell out of Chicago and going to a place where she was needed sounded even better. Hesitation coursed through her at the thought of marrying a stranger and sharing his bed as the woman in his world. She looked at the screen again. He wanted to talk. She wanted to talk to him as well but there was one other person she needed to speak to first.

Picking up her phone she punched in the number. She listened to the sounds of the rings on the other end then heard the click of connection. A breathy voice answered.

"Good morning, Coraline, I hope it's not too early. This is Khloe Burgess," she said into the phone.

"A fine morning it is Khloe, how's it going?"

"I've been corresponding with the Tennessee Mountain Man and he is ready for me to come on down and get this life together started," she said. "It is just so fast. I'm not sure."

"What are you uncertain about, Khloe? You have a 23 out of the 25-point match in personality, a 24 out of 25 matches in ideals, and on paper, sexually you are highly compatible," Coraline said.

"Yeah, but I don't know that man," she said honestly.

"That is what makes it wonderful," Coraline said. "I have seen people who have known each other for years marry and it all fall apart. My matches and marriages all stay together. We have only had two divorces in five generations."

"Are you saying that this is for real and that I should pack my shit and head to Tennessee and start a life with this man?"

"Why the hell not! You have nothing left for you in Chicago. Your job sucks and they don't respect the work you do," Coraline offered. "The one anchor you had is gone, and even your dog ran away. Get the hell out of town, go to him, and find your smile."

"Coraline, but what if I get there and he kisses like a baboon and his touch makes my skin crawl?"

"Highly doubtful," Coraline said, grinning in the phone. "He's a big man, but as gentle as a teddy bear."

"But, he just walked into your offices last week," Khloe said. "Off the street."

"As did you."

"Well, there is that," she countered.

"Khloe, I admit that normally we take months to vet a candidate, but I flew back with him to his home. I walked around his town, spent a few days in his world. There is nothing hidden," she said. "He didn't even call ahead to let anyone know we were coming. Well, he did call his folks because they don't like strangers, yet they were gracious people and his mother's biscuits melt in your mouth."

"My trust issues are red flagging my brain to say no," Khloe said.

"He is a Montgomery. In those parts, that name is a brand and it stands for something real to the locals and his family. If he is telling you that it is going to rain, then grab yourself an umbrella," Coraline said.

"His word is his bond," Khloe stated.

"His word is everything to that man. Get out of your own way, take this leap, and go and feel what it is like to be adored, loved, and the center of that man's world," she said.

"I am going to get all of that?'

"Darling, I think you are going to get a hell of a lot more," Coraline said, adding kisses into the line and hanging up.

Khloe looked about the house. It was still full of her mother's things. Plus, she needed to settle up with the insurance company on her home, the policies on her mother, and loads of details. 'Get out of your own way' Coraline had said. The phone still rested in the palm of her hand as her eyes went back to the screen and she punched in the number. Her heart thudded like she was running from the thugs who chased her last week. The pulse of blood through her veins raced to her heart as she listened to the sound of the rings, waiting for a connection. The line clicked and she stopped breathing.

"Beau Montgomery," the deep southern voice said.

"Good morning, this is Khloe Burgess," she said in a whoosh of words. *Be cool Khloe.*

"Hello, my lovely lady," he said as calmly as if they'd gone to see a movie last night and had tea afterward.

"Uhmm, I don't know where to start this conversation," she said.

"Then allow me," Beau said. "Khloe Burgess, marry me, be my life mate, pack up and come start a life with me."

"Well damn," she said, "that is one heck of a start."

"That is just the beginning," he told her. "I'm a man of few words. I have things to do on a daily basis and customers to serve. We are installing new computers and WiFi systems in the local school which is taking up almost every moment of my day. It starts to get cool in September in these parts but not like Chicago cold. These kids need shots before school starts back and I want to come home at night to a friendly face and tell you about my day and hear about yours over a modest meal before we call it a night. My life is simple. My request is simple. So, I ask you again, Khloe Burgess, marry me, pack up and come be the center of my world."

"Okay," she said, looking around the room as if another person had answered for her. "But Beau, we need to talk about things."

"Talk," he said.

"Kids, uhmm, sex, uhmm, we don't really know each other," she offered.

"You want kids right away?" he asked, surprised.

It was the way he said it which made her put on the *hold-up wait a minute brakes*. He didn't sound too enthusiastic over the idea. She wanted children and a family of her own.

Beau heard the silence, which slapped him across the nose like a bad dog who had chewed on his master's best shoes. "Khloe, I want a family as well, but if I had my way, waiting a year or two would be my preference, so we can get to know each other. It would kind of break my heart to bring kids into the marriage before you and I have a chance to settle into being us, before getting into a routine of taking care of them," he said.

"For a man of few words, you sure say a mouthful," she told him. "I am no spring chicken. I am pushing 40 and I don't want to sit at my kid's graduation looking like their grandmother."

"Understood, but I want our marriage to have every chance of surviving because we like each other," he said.

"Like each other?"

"Yeah, people get married because they fancy themselves in love. Love is grand and makes the heart go pitter patter, but friendship is what keeps people connected," he said.

She noticed that he avoided the sex portion of her fears in the earlier statement. That was the elephant eavesdropping on the call while munching on a barrel of peanuts. He needed to address that portion as well.

"The sex?"

"What about it?"

"Well, am I expected to fall into bed with you after we meet and marry?"

"Hell no," he said. "I don't know you like that."

He was laughing. A deep throaty laugh that warmed her all the way to her toes. She didn't find any humor at being sexually rejected over the phone and cleared her throat in protest.

"Khloe, my dearest Khloe. It would be unfair, in my estimation, to expect that from you right away. I want an intimate relationship. You can get sex or you can get intimacy. The latter sounds better to me. Besides, we need to get to know each other, get into a routine and get comfortable with being a man and a woman sharing a space. When it is time for our wedding night, we will have one. In the interim, we will focus on building our friendship, you getting going as the local...nurse?"

"Yes, I'm a Nurse Practitioner, but I have to get licenses to practice in Tennessee," she said.

"Tennessee is a part of the National Compact of Nursing Professionals. You can transfer your active license to this state and be all good," he said as a matter of fact and he heard her gulp. "My cousin, Jethro, who is the County Magistrate, looked it all up and gave me that info. You'll meet him when you arrive."

"Wait, where am I supposed to get medical supplies, vaccines and the lot?"

"Our last traveling physician was set up through a State Program, we can make some calls and get everything in order prior to your arrival," Beau told her. "How soon you planning to get here?"

"I have a few things to get settled on this end, so maybe two weeks?" she asked.

"Do you need me to fly in and help you drive down?"

"The solo ride will do me good," she said. "Give me a chance to swallow the craziness of my decision."

"It's not crazy at all, Khloe Burgess," he said. "Based on what Coraline has told me, we are a near perfect match. I've made my expectations very clear, and you want to find your smile. The past week I have spent thinking of ways to do just that."

"You are planning to help me find my smile?"

"I am planning to make you fall in love with me, woman," he said softly, "amongst other things, but yeah, when I'm done, you'll be grinning like you know things others have yet to discover and you will like me."

"Oh really," she said arching her brows as if he could see her facial expression through the phone.

"Really," he replied. "Come to me, Khloe."

"Okay," she said to the sultry southern voice that seemed to drain the logic from her brain. "What about my stuff?"

"Travel light to start," he said. "If you have loads of furniture, put it in storage until the spring. I will pay for the storage fees, then together we will travel to Chicago and bring it down."

"Dishes, pots and pans, towels, linens, that sort of thing?"

"Darling, I have the basics, but get here first and decide then what you need or may want based on the space," he said. "The house where we'll currently be living is kind of small, I'm pretty big, and I don't like clutter."

"Noted," she said. "Give me a week or so to finalize details on this end, and I will call you with a departure date."

"You sure you don't want me to fly in and help you out?"

"No, you have things to do on your end, with the school, my office, and the like," she said. "I got this end, you work on that one."

"Yes'um," he said grinning. "Call me every night just so I can hear your voice before I go to bed."

She inhaled sharply, surprised at how totally and ridiculously sexy that sounded to her. A man who actually wanted her to call him every night. Maybe this wasn't going to be so bad after all.

"Will do, Beau. Have a great day," she said.

"My day is getting better every second," he said before saying goodbye. He leaned back in the chair, putting his feet up on the desk and sighing deeply, satisfied with the conversation.

"That went better than I thought. You do have some game," a voice said, making Beau nearly jump out of the chair.

"Dammit, Jethro, how long have you been standing there?"

"Since you asked her to check the box that she liked you and wanted to go to Sally Hawkins dance as your date," Jethro said, chuckling.

"I still, really kind of hate you," Beau mumbled.

"That's fine, but I just got off the phone with Ennis, and he scored us a three-night stay at the beach on one of them time share thingies," Jethro said. "When's she coming so I can get it on my calendar and get the paperwork in order to pronounce you bear and lady bear."

"Two weeks," Beau said.

"Great, I need 50 bucks," Jethro said.

"For what?"

"I need to pay Jolene's daughter to go up to that tree house and scrub it from top to bottom, wash them pots like a woman would, and clean that bathroom real good," he said.

"My place is not dirty," Beau said with emphasis.

"It's not dirty by a man's standards, but will it pass a woman's inspection?" he asked, his bushy red eyebrows raised.

Beau took a $50 from his wallet and handed it to Jethro. "Just the girl. She can't bring any of her empty-headed friends," Beau said. "Oh hey, while I'm thinking about it, we need to get on the horn to the County Seat and get that office supplied for Khloe. She's a Nurse Practitioner."

"On it," Jethro said. "Let me know when she is planning to get here so I can have that gal clean the place. You want her to clean the office, too?"

Beau took out another $50 and placed it in Jethro's grubby paw. "Might as well," he said, taking a seat.

"You need a suit for the wedding," Jethro told him. "Call your sister to be the bridesmaid and witness, and I will get Jolene to do a small spread for the reception. Will your brother be the best man?"

"I have come to the conclusion, Jethro, that you don't have enough to do in this town," Beau said.

"Oh, I have plenty to do, but taking care of your big ass seems to be all I can get done," Jethro said. "Chop. Chop. We have a wedding to plan."

"Did I mention I kind of hate you?"

"Don't care none, but I do want you to like me. Our relationship has survived because you like me," Jethro said, mocking Beau's words to Khloe.

"Get out!" Beau roared.

He was down a $100 and half way pissed off because Jethro was once again right, plus he was going to get married. *Me. Married. Shit, this is actually happening.*

Beauregard Montgomery found himself smiling for the rest of the day.

THE NEXT TWO WEEKS zoomed by in a blur of activity with Khloe boxing up all of her mother's goods and the movers taking the bulk of it to storage. The dining room furniture—she knew her mother put it on lay-a-way, making bi-weekly payments in order to own nice things without a credit card bill — meant a great deal to Erica. It was the only furniture outside of her bedroom suit that her mother hadn't urinated on or worse. For that reason, it also held a value for Khloe, who stored it in a secure warehouse type of facility which was heated and air conditioned.

In the back of her mother's closet, she found a small strongbox secured by two locks. Unable to get either lock open, she loaded it into the back of her vehicle with a full set of Waterford China, crystal goblets, and silver dinner service along with the chargers, and the really nice Thanksgiving and Christmas tablecloths. Just because she was going to live on a mountain didn't make her mountainfolk and she had no intention of living like one. It was her hopes that in time, they would make friends to have over for dinner or if the occasion arose to entertain Beau's higher end clients, and there would be good china to serve their guests.

Clothing was rather scarce for Khloe since the fire, but she took a few pieces that remained at her mother's and the items she had left in her locker at work. The pride she felt when turning in her resignation to the snotty woman in HR nearly made her smile.

"Let us know if we can do anything for you, Ms. Burgess," Jennifer Conners told her. "I hope you are not leaving us out of spite."

"In order for me to be spiteful, that would indicate that I care what you think," Khloe said. "I don't. I'm getting married."

Before her work locker was empty, the buzz had encircled the ER, and the buzzards were encircling her like a piece of carrion to be fed upon. She wasn't having any part of it. Head held high, she waved farewell and stepped out into the night. Tonight, she planned to drive to at least Indianapolis and spend the evening there before driving on into Tennessee. For good measure, she placed a call to the only friend she had, Coraline.

"Hey, I'm leaving tonight for Tennessee, stopping in Indianapolis," she said. "I don't have any friends or family so to speak, and I just felt like someone other than Beau should know my plans."

"Good move, call me tonight when you check in and secure yourself a hotel room, then in the morning when you leave and again when you get to Harbuck," Coraline said.

"Thank you, this means a lot," Khloe said.

"Drive safe and be happy," Coraline said, disconnecting the call.

Beau didn't like the idea of her driving alone and reacted in a nurturing manner when she confessed to not having any family so to speak or friends. Calming words ensured Khloe that she shouldn't worry, that before the end of the year, as Mrs. Beauregard Montgomery there would be more friends and family than she could count. Taking him on his word, she rose early, left a message for Coraline, and drove most of the morning through one of the most painteresque landscapes she'd ever seen in her life. That was the word he used in his first letter. *Painteresque.* It was a good word to describe the lush green carpet of trees that covered the mountainside.

She shifted gears in the Jeep as she began the climb up the mountain into a flat patch of land that rolled into a jade covered field whispered to softly by the breezes which blew across the open grasses. The air felt different. The wind blowing across her skin seemed as if it were a split from the zephyrs that she inhaled in Chicago.

"I think I can be happy here," she said, pulling into the tiny town and locating the Courthouse that sat directly next to an empty office with a dark red medical cross on the window. On the opposite side of it sat an independent building with a satellite on the roof adorned with a large red, very masculine M. The painted-on sign in the window plainly displayed the name 'Montgomery Communications.'

This was it.

Her husband-to-be worked in that building. Quickly she made the call to Coraline, informing the matchmaker that she had in fact arrived in Harbuck. Next, she inhaled deeply and checked her teeth in the mirror for remnants of a hasty breakfast. Then, she checked her breath and just to play it safe, popped two breath mints into her mouth.

"Stop being an idiot, he's not going to kiss you," she admonished herself.

Inhaling deeply, she opened the door of the jeep, catching the attention of a few passersby. Head held high, expensive purse on her wrist, Khloe headed to the offices of Montgomery Communications, opening the door and letting herself in. A blond woman behind the desk looked up to see the tall Black woman standing in the office dressed as if she'd stepped off the pages of Life Styles of the Black and Famous. Her mouth hung open as her lips moved back in forth to find the words she wanted to say to Khloe.

"You lost?" the young woman asked.

"No, I'm here to see him," she said pointing to Beau, who had come out of the office and leaned against the door jamb. He'd seen the car pull in to town and park in front of the building. She was right on time. He liked that.

Khloe also liked what she saw. He was taller than she'd envisioned. The strawberry blonde hair was shaven on the sides of his head to display the scalp tattoos. Beau was a tough hombre to have his head needle punched with that much ink. He was attractive she noted as her eyes met his.

"Why do you need to see Mr. Montgomery?' the young girl asked.

"I came to marry him," Khloe said, waltzing past the woman towards Beau's office. She tugged on one of the buttons on the front of his shirt suggesting he follow her inside. He arched a single brow and looked at the receptionist before following behind his wife-to-be.

"Hold my calls, Sarah Jean," Beau said, closing his office door. He took a look at the tall ebony-skinned beauty and gave a low wolf whistle. "That photo did not do you justice. You sure you're in the right place?"

"If you are Beauregard Montgomery, then you are the right man and I am in the right place," she said, looking deep into the sultry green eyes.

"Sounds good. Get changed and we'll go get hitched."

"Wait...what?"

"I'll step out, you get changed, and we'll head over to the Courthouse and get this done," he said with a wink.

Then he left. She stood in the middle of the floor in his office, the room heavily laden with the scent of his woodsy cologne and his big manly chair. Khloe was confused.

"Hold up there, Mountain Man," she said, grabbing the door handle to find the large silhouette of him walking across the street.

"Beau said once you got dressed that I should come get him from the bar," Sarah Jean told her. "This is so exciting. Can I come to your wedding?"

Chapter Seven – Well, Do You?

Khloe wasn't getting changed or marrying anyone giving her orders with such highhanded tactics. That may have worked for him as the owner and boss man of his little communications company up in the mountains, but it didn't work for her. If he took to drinking in the middle of the day, then she would drive herself back to Chicago and live in a hotel until she figured out what was next. She did match with the man in Arizona and the apple grower in Vermont. There were choices other than the burly brute.

Leaving an open-mouthed Sarah Jean to call behind her yelling, "Wait, pretty Black lady!" Khloe marched across the street to the Whistle Wetter Bar and Café, which was just a diner that sold liquor shots. Beau sat on one of the four bar stools at the counter, swirling dark liquor in a glass. Khloe took a seat beside him, looking at the gal behind the counter who stood frozen gawking at her.

"Brandy please," she told the woman. "Is this a habit of yours, drinking in the middle of the day?"

"No, I just needed to calm my nerves," he said, clenching his hand around the semi-clean glass. Khloe nodded to the girl behind the counter, thanking her for the drink which had been placed upon the counter.

"If you are having second thoughts, let me know. There will be no hard feelings," she said.

Beau picked up the glass, gazing at the brown contents, wanting to gulp it down in one swallow, but she needed to know where he was in his head. The last thing he wanted her to do was leave. All morning he'd been on pins and needles worried she would chicken out and not come, yet when he saw the silver Rubicon roll down the street and park, he knew it was her. His mail-order bride had come, not via wagon train, but a 285-horse powered Jeep engine. Unable to take his eyes off the car, when the door opened and that long leg attached to the cute sexy sandal-covered foot touched the ground, he nearly squealed in delight. Her thick head of curly hair and the ebony skin made him long for the wedding night he promised her they would wait to have. The picture didn't do her justice. She was downright pretty. And here to marry him.

"If you look at your life as if it were a large puzzle, logically, you would start by sorting out the pieces, finding the edges to make a frame," he told her. "As you come back to the pile of pieces, the search begins for patterns and shapes to make the image come to life. Over time, all the pieces come together until that last little section, which is intricate in detail, and needs to be put together in a certain order."

He looked at her. The smooth dark skin begged him to touch her, caress the softness which oozed from the pores and nurture the unsmiling woman inside. The deep brown eyes looking at his mouth as he said the words. Her eyes finally meeting his.

"You are the last piece," he said. "I feel luckier than a pig in mud on a hot August day and my hands can't stop shaking. Lady, you are one amazing package. Please tell me you aren't crazy, on medication for bipolar disorder, or have a truck full of cats or garden gnomes with stupid names."

"Well, when you walked out of your office and left me standing there like an idiot, I started to believe I was nuts," she said, "but no, I'm not on any regular medication. Bi-polar either, and I'm allergic to cats. The garden gnome thing might be cute once I see the garden but I did bring a good set of china and tablecloths for the holidays. I wasn't sure if you entertained big clients so I wanted to have fancy dishes to make a grand impression."

"You made a grand impression on me when you walked into my offices and told my assistant you'd come to marry me," he said. "I didn't know whether to kiss you or club you across the head and drag your feet first to the Courthouse."

Khloe's lips began to twitch, wiggling back and forth as if she were trying to tie a cherry stem with her tongue. She pressed them together to stop the action so he wouldn't think she had a form of Tourette's.

"What are you doing with your mouth?"

"I think my lips were trying to form a smile, but it felt weird," she said. "I made it stop."

Beau burst into laughter. A deep, hearty chest laugh and for the life of her, she wanted to lean her head against his chest to hear it up close. A gentle giant Coraline had said.

"This is gonna be good," he said, smiling at her. The poker face gave back no reaction but her eyes said it all. He would learn to read those eyes as they became comfortable with each other. "You bring a dress to get hitched in?"

"I have an appropriate dress in the car," she said.

"Well, we don't want to keep the Magistrate waiting since we have an appointment," Beau told her. "Grab your things, head into my office, and get dolled up, and I will come for you...no wait. I'm not supposed to see you before the wedding, right?"

"In this case, we will be okay," she said.

"No, don't want to jinx my luck. I'll have Sarah Jean accompany you over," he said. "I have my jacket and tie over there in my office. Let me get that while you get your suitcase."

"You're used to giving orders, aren't you?"

"Yeah, you used to following' em?"

"No, I'm used to giving them as well," she said. "A few adjustments are going to be needed on both our parts. I don't blindly follow orders. 'Please' and 'thank you' work well with me, Beauregard Montgomery."

He was smiling again. A big toothed, well maintained, pearly white smile of a man who took care of his teeth. That was a plus, she thought.

"Yes'm," he said. "Will you please go get your shit and get dolled up for me so I can slip a ring on that finger and call you mine from this day forward?"

"Sure, right after you go and put on that necktie so I can yank on it every time you forget to say please and thank you," she told him, squinting under his gaze.

He started laughing again.

"I don't know about making you smile, but dang gummit, I sure as hell am smiling more today that I have in the last year," he said, raising his glass. "A toast to us."

Khloe raised her glass as well, repeating, "To us."

A clink of dirty glasses sealed the deal as both threw back the contents of the glasses, wiped their mouths, and exhaled deeply. He offered her his arm, which she accepted, and they walked across the street to her car. A valise and a dress bag in hand, she went inside the office and changed into the simple white dress and added a strand of pearls and high heeled white pumps.

Sarah Jean waited for her, snapping photos with her phone, chatting 50 miles a minute about not seeing a Black person up close before. She thanked Khloe for being so nice, then asked how she and her boss met, if she lived in a ghetto and was escaping a rough life in the projects to come live in fresh air.

"Darling," Khloe said to Sarah Jean. "I'm pretty nervous as is and you aren't helping any."

"Sorry," Sarah Jean said as she opened the door to the small Courthouse and led Khloe down a small hall into the Office of the Magistrate.

A man with hair so red he looked like Heat Miser, sat behind a desk. Beau was not in the room, and a wave of panic overcame her. The baby's breath in her hair fell down over her eyes, making her fumble to get it back in place.

"I got that," Sarah Jean said. "Ooh, your hair is so soft, like cotton balls. I thought it would be brittle and dry."

Khloe gave her a sister girl look of *sit yo ass down*, but she needed a friendly face. Sarah Jean was all she had. Her vision blurred a tad and her legs felt wobbly. The man with the ridiculous red hair was at her side, holding her by the elbow.

"Get her some water, Sarah Jean," the man said. "I am Jethro Montgomery, the Magistrate, and your soon-to-be cousin-in-law. Beau is in the other room waiting for you, along with a bridesmaid and a few wedding guests. Let me know when you are ready to go in."

"Thank you," she said. "I just need a moment and a bite to eat – feeling a bit lightheaded."

"We have vittles for after the nuptials," Jethro said. "Jolene over at the diner put together a nice little spread."

Sarah Jean handed her the water, and she sipped greedily wishing she hadn't drunk the brandy on an empty stomach. Jethro, she thought that was his name, got her up on wobbly legs and moving towards another room. He tapped on the door three times, and a bigger red headed version of the Magistrate came out of the room.

"Oh shit," Khloe said taking a step back.

"This here's my Pa, Big Red. He is going to escort you down the aisle since your Pap ain't here," Jethro informed her, placing her hand on the big man's arm as he clapped his hands, calling everyone to places. Music started in the background making her head snap around to locate the intrusive sound.

Khloe had never heard Mendelssohn's Wedding March played on a banjo before. The crisp clear sound filled the small room, neatly decorated with paper wedding bells and a food table covered in a white tablecloth. An older woman with graying hair that used to be almost honey blond stepped forward.

"Dearie, you need something blue," the lady said. "Here, take my handkerchief which will serve as your something old, borrowed, and blue."

"Thank you so much," Khloe said, accepting the token.

Beauregard waited for her as she walked down the created aisle on what appeared to be a laid out roll of family size white paper towels. She wouldn't complain, at least someone had made the effort to make the Courthouse wedding ceremony as pretty as they could. *For this, Oh Lord, I give thanks.*

She reached the front of the room to stand beside her groom-to-be. To his right stood an older and smaller replica of the man she was marrying, minus a full set of teeth. He frowned at Khloe as her mouth twitched again in an effort to form a smile. It didn't work.

On her left stood a sandy red-headed woman who said, "Hey Gurl, let's do this!"

"Okaaay," Khloe said as she faced forward, looking at the man named Jethro. She blinked several times realizing he was also going to marry her and Beau.

"Who gives this woman in matrimony?" Jethro asked.

"I guess that's me, but she ain't really mine to give," Big Red said.

"Pa, just say it's you," Jethro scolded.

"Fine, here, take her," Big Red said, giving her a small push in Khloe's back. "I don't know her no how!"

"Pa, just sit down," Jethro said.

"You may be the Magistrate, and I still don't know what that means other than you've turned into Mr. Bossy Britches," Big Red said to his son, "but that don't make you the boss of me! I'm still your Pappy!"

"Yes'sir, Pap, but will you please take a seat?" Jethro asked changing his tone.

"I'm sitting down 'cause my knees a'aching, not 'cause you told me to," Big Red said, brushing his thumb across his nose like a martial arts fighter in a Bruce Lee film. As long as he didn't yell, "Right! Get her!" Khloe was fine. Her eyes focused on the man about to marry her to Beau.

"We are gathered here today to join Khloe Reneta Burgess to our very own Beauregard Sherman Montgomery in holy matrimony," Jethro said.

The woman with graying honey blond hair wailed as Khloe turned around. Both the bridesmaid, the replica of Beauregard, and the man himself all said in unison, "Ma!"

"Sorry, he just looks so handsome and she looks like a skinny black baby doll," Honey said. "I just want to kiss her and play with her hair."

Khloe's hands fisted in an effort to hold onto the sweat balls forming in her palms as Jethro cleared his throat.

"Do you, Khloe Burgess, take this man, to be your lawfully wedded husband, of your own free will and volition, and no one has pressured you into doing so," Jethro asked.

"I guess...I do," Khloe said.

"You can't guess and just say I do," Jethro instructed. "You have to repeat the words verbatim."

"Oh, for the sake of Jesus' blood, Jethro, you are taking this job of yours too serious," the replica of Beau said.

"She has to repeat the words as I have instructed," Jethro said, sticking out his chest. "Now, Ms. Burgess, please repeat the words."

Exhaling, she turned to Beau. "I, Khloe Renata Burgess, take you, Beauregard Sherman Montgomery, to be my lawfully wedded husband, of my own free will, and volition and no one has pressured me into doing such."

"Thank you. Now you, Beau," Jethro said.

"I do," he said.

"Beau, you have to repeat it as it was said unto you," Jethro demanded.

"Stop being a donkey's ass, Jethro, and let's get this over and done," Beau countered.

"Ooh girl, he is anxious to get to that treehouse," her bridesmaid said.

The Beau replica leaned around his brother, "Yeah, it's been a while for him. He is going to wear your ass out tonight."

Beau elbowed him in the stomach as Jethro called for the rings. He handed one to Khloe who refused it and took a string from the inside of her dress which held a silver-toned ring. Steady hands undid the knot, freeing the platinum band with one shiny citrine in the middle. She slid it upon his left ring finger and he slid one similar onto her hand with a red ruby in the middle.

"I got you a ring because I didn't think you knew the size of his bear paw," Jethro said.

"No, I have it covered," Khloe responded.

"Good. Good," Jethro replied. "By the power vested in me by the Commonwealth of Tennessee, I now pronounce you man and wife. You may kiss your bride."

The banjo player began picking as Beau lowered his head, his lips touching Khloe's, his hands at his side. She pressed her mouth to his, feeling sparks shoot down her sides before he pulled away. The bridesmaid, as Khloe turned, slapped her in the face with a handful of rice.

"Damn," Khloe said, brushing the hard grains out of her hair and nose.

"You are going to clean that up, Katy Mae Montgomery," Jethro said, pointing at the rice grains on the floor.

"Am not," she said. "What are you going to do, write me a citation for rice throwing?"

"Cut it out, all of you," Beau said. "Khloe, this part of my family. My mother, Honey, my sister Katy Mae, this here is my brother, Lil Bo', you met my Uncle, Big Red, and our Magistrate, Jethro Montgomery."

"Pleasure to meet you all," she said.

"Hugs. Hugs, and pictures," Honey called out, snapping photos with her phone. No one had a camera, but they all had phones, so lights flashed, and the banjo player decided to pull out his repertoire of fun family songs. He was picking and everyone was grinning. The chaffing dishes were uncovered with foods Khloe was surprised she recognized. Of course, there was a hearty helping of fried chicken, what looked like collard greens loaded with chunks of pork fat, cornbread, and what she assumed were chitterlings. All the things she didn't eat.

Khloe was grateful for the crudités which is what she snacked on. Honey, who had been dying to get her alone, sidled up to her. "I know you lost your Ma, but if we need to talk about what happens on the wedding night, I'm here for you," Honey said.

"I think I'll be able to figure it out," Khloe said, looking in the same green eyes she'd gifted to her son.

"Good for you," Honey said, giving Khloe the side eye. "Can I touch your hair?"

"No," Khloe said, trying to give the woman a smile.

"What is wrong with your lips, you having a conniption fit or somethin'?" Honey asked. "My cousin, Francine, I think she had a penis allergy. Every time her husband would mention it was sexy time, her lips would twitch like that too. Are you afraid of Beau's penis?"

"No ma'am, I was trying to give you a smile in my refusal of your offer to play in my hair. It is offensive to a Black woman to ask such a liberty," Khloe said. "And, please, talking about your son's penis is uncomfortable."

"Well, will Beau be able to yank on it when you're celebrating your nuptials? Your hair, not his penis, I mean. It won't come out like one of them waves," Honey said.

"I think you mean weaves. No, this is my hair," she said, maintaining the poker face she was known for.

"Lordy be, I may need to let Beau know he can't play with your hair," she said to Khloe.

"He can play with it any time he likes, just not you or your family," Khloe told her. "It would greatly be appreciated if you spread the word."

"Of course," Honey said, patting her hand. She turned to the small group. "Everyone, no one can play in Khloe's hair but Beau, so don't ask. It's offensive to Black women. Spread the word."

Three people said aww and two others groaned as she looked at her new husband, whose cheeks were red as fire. Katy Mae bragged about the fried chicken and mustard greens as she loaded up plates for Khloe and Beau to take home to eat on after the hard loving they would have tonight.

"Add some of my biscuits and jam with them plates, Katy Mae," Honey called out.

"Already did Ma," the girl called back. "Khloe asked Beau for my cell number and call me if you need anything."

"I appreciate it," Khloe said.

"It can get lonely in these parts, especially during the Winter, although I know you are going to be busy with the clinic and all. There are at least three people up in them hills with a rash that won't go away who will be your first customers," she said with a lopsided grin.

"Glad I will at least have clients," she said to her sister-in-law.

"Oh, you're gonna have lots of clients and loads to do," Katy Mae said. "Welcome to the family."

The banjo player eased out of the music as everyone gathered around by the door. Khloe prayed she wasn't going to get slapped in the face with more rice as hand-in-hand she and her new husband walked down the line of Montgomerys into their new life together as husband and wife.

"Lil' Bo, pick me up in the morning for work," Beau told his brother, then to Khloe he said, "We'll drive your car to the house."

The seat had to be pushed back as far as it could go to accommodate the height of the man she now called husband. Seated inside the Jeep next to him, looking down at the wedding ring, nervousness creeped inside of her. He said no wedding night, but the way he looked at her made her think the big man had changed his mind.

"Give me your phone," he said to Khloe. Before he had time to react she had his necktie in her hand, pulling his face close to hers and nearly choking him. He offered her a grin before rephrasing his request, "May I have your phone please so I can program the GPS coordinates in for the house?"

"Certainly, husband," she said, releasing the tie with a light kiss on the tip of his nose, then handed him her cell phone. It was a small gesture of affection, but she needed to get comfortable with him. If she gave affection early, Khloe hoped he would give it back in vast quantities.

Instead of him being angry, he burst into laughter again. "Dang it, woman, I am liking you more and more by the minute," he said, starting the Jeep, shifting the gears, and taking them to her new home.

They rode in silence through the mountains and she was grateful he'd plugged in the coordinates. If she had to find it on her own, Khloe would be lost in the woods. They came to a clearing, made a sharp turn, headed down a slope, rounded a bend and came to what he said was home.

"What the hell is that?" she asked, leaning out the window to look at what would be her domicile.

"Welcome home, darling," he said with a proud grin.

Chapter Eight – It's Simple. I Like It.

She stared at the structure, trying in her best estimation to create a description of what she was seeing. It reminded her of a treehouse stuck in the side of a hill. The more she looked at it, the more it resembled a wooden yurt on stilts. There were no stairs so she couldn't quite figure out how to get inside her new home. The good news was that it had loads of windows. The bad news was that the only thing she would be able to see out of them would be the trees.

"What is it?" she asked, trying to open the door. Beau's hand reached over, touching her arm sending little sparks down to her toes.

"Not yet, this is just the front, we have to drive around back and up the hill to get inside," he said, shifting to a low gear and rolling the Jeep forward.

It was a slow climb over compacted soil. Her eyes remained focused on the wooden beams holding her new home up in the air. Although she'd researched the rainfall in the area, a good earthquake would shake them from the sky into a slow rolling death down the mountain. His hand was still on her arm as the vehicle climbed higher, coming the rear of the structure. Beau placed the Jeep in park and cut the engine.

"This is my hunting cabin," he said. "Working down at the school, it is easier to get back and forth to town as well as the sunlight here is great for the garden."

"Oh yeah, the garden," she said, absently gawking at the hexagon-shaped structure.

"Grab your stuff and get changed. We have a lot to get done before the sun sets," he said but found himself moving quickly to avoid her grabbing his necktie. She'd reached for it, but he was quick for a man of his size. However, he wasn't quick enough to avoid her grabbing his belt buckle and yanking his body with some force into the side of the car. His chest hit the door opening, and he grunted.

"Mrs. Montgomery," he said, amused at how quickly she moved as well. "Time is of the essence. Will you please grab a suitcase to change your clothing so I can show you how this works before the sun goes down?"

"Mr. Montgomery, I can do that. Thank you for asking so nicely," Khloe said, letting go of his belt buckle.

Beau moved gingerly around the car to open the door for her. Her long legs sent his imagination into overdrive and he averted his glance to the back of the vehicle. Three boxes, two suitcases, and a strongbox. He would bring those in later. Khloe moved around him to open the rear passenger door to collect her purse, valise, and the smaller of the cases. Her small rounded bottom stuck in the air as she grabbed the case, and for the life of him, he wanted to take hold of those hips and pull them against his own just to ensure a snug fit. *Focus, man.*

Suitcase in one hand and valise in the other, she let out a small whoop when he lifted her in his strong arms and threw her over his shoulder. She held tightly to the baggage as he carried his bride inside the structure. When he set his wife down on her feet she saw that the house was bigger on the inside than she'd imagined.

"It has walls," she said.

"The house also has a water closet for guests and a master bath," he said. "If you please, Mrs. Montgomery, let's start there."

The master bedroom didn't hold much furniture outside of a corner bureau with six drawers. A king-sized bed, with a nightstand on either side and three small closets, made up the master sleeping quarters. *It is quaint.*

"We have a tub and a stand-up shower, through there," he said, pointing at the door. Beau then took her focus to the outside. The master bedroom had two sliding glass doors. One set led to an open deck. The other set led to a screened-in porch. "If you like that sort of thing, we have a hot tub outside for soaking."

"I like that sort of thing," she said, touching his arm. His eyes followed her fingers, loving the tender touch of the warm digits on his tattooed arms.

"I'll change in the other room, while you change in here. Please come out when you are ready," he said. "The two closets on the left are yours."

"Thank you," she said softly, taking her valise into the bathroom. To her amazement, there were two vanities. The one with the larger mirror, and nothing on the counter, she assumed was hers. Getting out of the dress, she changed into a pair of leggings, a loose fitted blouse, and a pair of sneakers. She nearly smiled when she noticed the bathtub had jets. *At least he's not a barbarian.*

Changed and ready to see what the evening would bring, she went out on the deck to look at the hot tub. It was large enough for four. To her left, she went through a door which took her to the screened-in porch where, to her delight, baskets of hanging berries and fruit that grew plump and ready for plucking dangled. There were fruit trees in planters that grew oranges, avocados. and lemons. Another set of glass doors led her into the main living area.

Khloe stepped through the doors and sighed in relief. A love seat and couch resided in front of a fireplace and a flat screen television hung above it. The coffee table, a chunk of a tree trunk with a perfectly rounded piece of glass, held a small planter of lavender in the center. A bookcase, just the right size, held two shelves of books. Two others were empty for her to add to the collection. Sliding glass doors sat to the left and right of the fireplace.

The open space of the home was refreshing. In the dining area, a rounded table, cut from the trunk of a what appeared to be the same tree, showcased the age of the fallen oak. Highly polished and sparkling like glass, the base, still in its natural form with bark, was covered in a poly-urethane which also made it shine. Eight chairs sat around the table and as for a dining room, it worked. The low credenza stuck in the angled wall made the cabinet unit appear to be a built-in. Khloe thought it would be perfect to showcase the china she'd brought with her. The glass door, delicately inserted, was clear enough to display the Wedgewood. Evidently, Beau thought so as well because the box of china she'd brought sat in front of it.

"Later," she said. "You can put those away later."

To the right of the credenza, was another set of glass doors which led to an outdoor grill. It looked like an outdoor kitchen shoved into the side of the hill.

"Nice," she said, looking at the small but totally adorable kitchen. The island, which also served as a room divider between the kitchen and dining table, also held a sink. The kitchen, while not very large, held a dorm sized fridge, a four-burner stove and an edible garden in hanging baskets that grew above the sink nestled inside the two windows. A larger window was set over the sink, giving her a view of the mountains, which made her breath catch.

A sound drew her gaze as Beau came out of a room. Curiosity made her wander over to see what was in it, and she passed the water closet to enter a small office. The walls were bookshelves from the floors to the ceiling that held books of all sorts.

"Wow," she said.

"I take it that means you like your new home?" he asked, watching her with interest.

"It's simple, yet thoughtfully put together. I like," she said, looking over her shoulder at him. "The edible garden in the kitchen is amazing. Where do you get your power and water?"

"Glad you asked," he said. "We are solar powered with a backup generator. It helps to charge your devices at night and pace yourself during the day on power usage. The water comes from rain, which in this location we don't get much because of the mountain, and the rest comes from a nearby reservoir."

"So, water is plenty," she said.

"No, not really," Beau replied. "Showers need to be quick. I recycle the water through triple filtration on two areas of inflow and outflow. The outflow is used to water the garden, which is our primary source of food."

"Oh great, lettuce which tastes like soap," she said.

"The filters are changed every three months to prevent that," he said. "I don't want to eat my dead skin cells."

"I really appreciate that," she said, looking into the green eyes. Beau blinked several times before reaching for her hand. She placed it inside of his as he led her to the living room. A large cabinet rested against the wall that backed against the closets in their bedroom.

"Under here are weapons," he said. "I need to take you out and see you shoot to make sure you can handle every piece under there."

"Beau, I was in the Army for 20 years. I am a soldier. I can fire a weapon," she said.

"Yeah, but you were a nurse," he said. "Your main weapons were a syringe and a bedpan."

"Ah, so we have jokes," Khloe said.

"Evidently, they weren't funny enough to make you smile," he said. "I look forward to hearing, at some point, what robbed you of your joy."

"Life sucked it out of me. End of story," she said, bending over to give him another view of the delicious handful of butt. "Let's see what you have under there."

Beau pulled out a Beretta, a .9mm Colt, a six-shooter, a Taurus Judge, a .45 Colt Revolver, three rifles, and a shotgun.

"Well damn, thinking of starting your own militia?" she asked, fingering the weapons.

"These are the law up here," he said to her. "If a bear comes through that glass, you have to be ready. Mountain lions are also in these parts and meth dealers. I have to travel a bit some days to serve my customers. There will be times when you will travel with me, and other times, you may be here alone. I have to know you can handle yourself."

"I can handle anything that comes my way," she said confidently.

"Yeah, you can," he said. "You're handling me just fine."

There it was again. That look. The words of his brother came to her, "He's going to wear your ass out tonight." Her hands fisted and opened in nervousness at the thought.

"Come o...," he started but stopped himself. "Wife, we need to do few target practice shots, then I need to show you the garden before we can have some supper and settle in for the night."

"Wife. Woman. You can simply call me, Khloe," she said, touching his arm.

"Been alone a long time. I have to say the words to remind myself that it's no longer just me. I have a woman to come home to, to see about and nurture. I have a wife who needs her man. Mrs. Montgomery exists in my world and saying the words makes you, this, us real," he said, collecting the shotgun, rifle, and six-shooter. "Shall we go outside and see what you're made of."

The target range was under the stilts of the house. It was a large cut of the same tree that made up the coffee and dining room tables. From the look of the wood, the same tree could have easily been the parent of the bookshelves, credenza, and cabinets. She made a mental note to ask him as they climbed down a deep set of steps. The wood blocks, surrounded by loose rocks, made a pathway of steps down under the house. A table rested far enough away to hold the weapons, but it was covered in spider webs. He used a brush to whisk them all away.

"Wife, it becomes a matter of life and death to dust frequently and move the cobwebs away inside the home," he said. "Simple, intricate webs belong to our spider friends who keep the pests away. Crazy webs belong to poisonous spiders who will rot your skin."

"Brown recluses and black widows," she said.

"There are also brown widow spiders who make pretty webs, but don't trust them either," he said. "Let's get in some shots, then head back up to the garden before it gets dark."

He handed her the six-shooter and a box of rounds. Khloe loaded the weapon, aimed at the target, and fired six shots dead center.

"Impressive," he said, handing her the .9mm. She slapped in the cartridge, racking the slide to pull a round into the chamber, squeezing the trigger and repeated the same perfect shots, center mass. Before he could say any more, she loaded the rifle, fired three rounds in the same center. Then Khloe reached for the shotgun, but his fingers pressed against the soft flesh of her hand, preventing contact the weapon.

"Show off," he said with a smile.

"When I tell you, I can do a thing," she said, "I can do a thing."

"So, I see," he said. "Up next, Wife, is the garden. I hope you can do a weeding thing because your husband hasn't had time."

They climbed the steps to the deck, rounding the hot tub to a dip in the hillside. She inhaled sharply at the size and variety of the raised bed garden that had PVC pipes running horizontally through the rows.

"That's some garden," she said. The bedding wasn't too bad and chicken wire surrounded the wooden boxes.

"Rabbits think so as well. The rabbits bring the foxes and bobcats," he said, "and the woodrats bring the copperheads and timber rattlers, so always wear thick boots with heavy socks when you work out here."

"It doesn't look too bad. The weeding I mean."

"Maybe, but usually it looks better than this," he said. "This garden is currency. It is how we buy meats and others items we need for the winter."

"Excuse me?"

"The ad specified a knowledge of gardening," he said. "I hope you also know how to can and store veggies. My folks hold an Autumn Equinox Festival that is coming up in two weeks. They call it a festival because a few of the cousins bring ponies for the kids to ride, but my folks slaughter a few hogs. We trade the vegetables for a ham, bacon, pork butts, and the like. A few folks have beef, but I travel enough to hit a grocery store to get mine. People will pay you in what they have. Arts, crafts, possum pies...most folks don't have money."

"Wait... did you just say possum pie?"

"Yeah, it's like chicken pot pie but made with possum," he said. "Some are pretty tasty but my Ma makes the best."

She stood staring at him, her face expressionless which made him start to laugh. That deep throaty laugh followed by the rumbling of his belly. It was the cue to head inside for the evening as the sun began to dip low behind the hills and darkness settled in around them like a mist.

INSIDE, HE SET THE table with two plates, two forks, and two glasses. The refrigerator didn't make ice, which he said was a luxury item. The food he warmed on the top of the stove and plated for them to sit and enjoy.

"I know it's not the ideal wedding night or nuptial meal but as soon as the school is done, we will take a honeymoon," he told her.

"Compared to the war zone I just left, the peace and quiet of this is honeymoon enough," she said, taking his hand and asking him to bow his head for prayer.

Khloe didn't remember the last time she had fried food let alone fried chicken, and she ate it like an inmate fresh out the pen. The chitterlings she refused to eat and found the greens edible. Honey Montgomery's biscuit melted in her mouth and she sat licking the crumbs off her finger.

"Don't eat often?"

She chuffed, almost offering a smile. "I eat several times per day, but not fried foods," she said, looking up at him. "Haven't had fried chicken in years, but I'm curious, was this meal planned for my palate?"

"Are you asking if they cooked fried chicken, mustard greens, and chit'lin's cause you're Black? Hell no, this is every day eating for us," Beau said.

"Oh wow," she replied, eyeing the second piece of chicken that he slid across the table for her to have. "This leads me to another question. You specified a Black woman. Any reason why or you had an experience in college that you never got over?"

"Naw," he said. "It was Penny."

Khloe ripped the chicken wing apart, nibbling on the flat portion, sucking the meat from the bone. "Who is Penny?"

"The girl from *Good Times*," he said, sucking the chicken grease off his finger.

"Janet Jackson?"

"Noooo, there is a difference, between sweet little Penny and Janet," he said. "I fell in love with Penny."

"This I have to hear," she said, leaning forward, hanging on his every word. Beau took her plate, scraping off the chitterlings and adding them to his own, and passing her the last chicken thigh. She thanked him, continuing to eat the greasy yard bird, praying it didn't tear her stomach up.

"My Pa, you'll meet him soon, has always given me a wide berth because he said I was real smart. One summer, I asked to go to the beach. We went, but keep in mind my folks are simple people," he said. "No hotel rooms or anything like that, so he called it camping. That meant all of us would sleep in the back of the truck with a tarp over it to avoid skeeter bites."

Khloe sat expressionless wondering where he was going with the story, but she listened, just enjoying the imagery he painted with his words.

"We get to the beach in North Carolina and there are these Black kids, first time I ever seen any up close," he said. "They lived on the beach in a house that their parents owned. Even had a colored television in the house."

"You guys didn't own a television?"

"Yeah, we did, but Pa gutted it and made it into a fish tank," he said.

"Well, that's progressively artistic," she said.

Beau shook his head no. "Pa ain't nothing like that. He gutted the tv, lined it and put pond water in it to store his catch. In the mornings when he wanted fish and grits, he would walk by the tank and reach in and grab his breakfast."

The corners of Khloe's mouth begin to move as her lips tried to form a smile. She thought better of it, not wanting to laugh at her husband's father. Instead, she pressed her lips together.

"Okay, back to Penny," she said.

"Oh yeah, Penny," he said, forking in a hearty helping of the chitterlings into his mouth. "These kids were watching *Good Times* and in entered little Penny. I thought she was the most beautiful thing I had ever seen in my life. Well, until dude, Rodney I think his name was, that's who I was hanging with that day - his sister Shanté walked through the living room in a swimsuit. That was the first time in my whole existence I saw an ass that wasn't flat."

Khloe sputtered.

"It was round, had no jiggle when she walked and peeking out from under that swimsuit making my 12-year-old pecker poked up in my pants," he said. "Shanté thought it was cute and asked me to follow her to the back room. She made a mistake that day."

Khloe became concerned that her husband had done a bad thing. The expression of worry showed on her face. Beau only gave her a knowing look.

"Oh, weren't nothing like that," he said with a wink. "It was some of that, but a 12-year-old mountain boy ain't nothing like a 15-year-old city boy. I showed her things her body could do that she would have learned in college from a Senior Biology major."

"At 12? How old was she?"

"About 15 or so, but when I was done with her, she possessed the knowledge of a 21-year-old," he said, laughing. "That damned gal followed me around all weekend. Thus, began my love of Black women."

"And here we are," she said.

"Here we be," he replied, rising to collect the dishes. "I wash, you dry?"

"Sure," she said, looking around the place as she stood beside him. "Are we sharing the bed tonight?"

"No, too soon. I'll take the couch," he said.

Khloe eyed the couch, which wasn't long enough for him to sleep on comfortably. Swallowing hard, she touched his arm.

"I'll take the couch, you keep your bed. You have to go to work in the morning," she said.

"Hell, so do you," he told her. "That garden needs to be weeded, the vegetables harvested then canned. You are in control of our books and the meat larders. I can go a few days without meat, but if you want eggs and honey, plus more of my Ma's jam, those vegetables are important."

"A mate, huh?" she asked with her lips twisted in distaste.

"Right now, it sounds as if I needed a farm hand, but when the time comes, you will see the value as well as importance," he told her.

"Beau, what about the office, when do I start there?"

"Monday," he said. "Jethro will have all the supplies in by then. Plus, I will have put in the new locks, and this weekend, we get to spend some time together."

"Sounds like a plan," she said, starting the dishwater.

He was staring at her again. That hungry look was in his eyes like he wanted to pull a Shanté on her body and motorboat her butt cheeks. Khloe moved closer to him, wrapping her arms around his neck. Tiptoeing just an inch or so, she initiated a real kiss.

Damn you, Shanté, she thought to herself. The man kissed like the only thing left to do was poke her with his finger and she would be sated and slobbering on a pillow. Her body reacted to him in a way she hadn't experienced in a long time as she pressed closer to him, trying to determine how long the pole was she would use to vault her to Happy Land.

Beau pulled away.

"We have time," he said. "Let's take it. I want to be more than just the man in your bed, Khloe."

At this point, he could be any damned thing he wanted to be. She liked Beauregard Montgomery more and more each minute she spent in his company. The family gave her reservations, but in time, all things would balance out.

Chapter Nine – Pa, Sis, and a Jethro.

The let-out bed was far more comfortable than she'd expected as she settled in, nestling her head into the pillows. What she did find uncomfortable was the amount of darkness that encircled the house like a well-fitted glove on a large hand. The blackness leaned against the glass sliding doors like a voyeur trying to see into a human habitat. It creeped her out to think that maybe, just outside taking a sip in the hot tub water, was a bobcat. She pulled the covers up under her chin, then over her head.

Stop being a wimp. You served tours in Bosnia and Iraq and two in Afghanistan. Hell, you lived in Chicago and worked in a hospital that seemed to feed the bank account of the County Mortician. It's just darkness.

Sighing deeply, her mind went over her day. The drive. Meeting her husband in person. Getting married. Walking down the aisle over a paper towel white carpet and eating fried chicken and mustard greens for her wedding night meal. A wedding night where she slept on the couch and all that bear of a man slept alone in the next room in that big ol' bed, all by his lonesome. Her body hummed from the thought of his kisses, reminding her that she and that idiot Joey hadn't been intimate in a very long while, and the last time they did, it was rushed. She'd barely gotten there when he'd grunted, humped, and slumped over her like he'd done a 12-hour shift in a coal mine. It was doubtful that her husband would be so lackadaisical about taking care of her needs in bed.

Holding on to that thought, she drifted off to sleep.

IN THE NEXT ROOM, BEAU lay flat on his back staring at the ceiling, calling himself all sorts of morons and idiots for suggesting they take their time. In his heart, he knew it was the right thing to do. His private parts disagreed with him wholeheartedly by making a tent in the sheet, egging him to go in the other room, pick up her, and bring her into this bed.

She is pretty awesome. The whole not smiling thing is kind of creepy. Who doesn't smile? It's like she'd forgotten how and the muscles that activated the lips for the function had atrophied in place, leaving her stuck with resting bitch face. Dang gone she is a pretty little chocolate thing. Our kids are going to be gorgeous. Heads full of wavy or curly hair. Intense eyes.

Then, out a nowhere, a vision of a little girl with caramel colored skin, hazel eyes, and jet-black hair flashed before his eyes. The tent-maker subsided as a soft, squishy feeling hit him in the chest. A frilly pink dress with red bows and shiny white shoes with a little sunbonnet adorned the child's head as she called out to him, her arms held high for him to lift her up and smother her adorable face with kisses. The vision stayed with him as he drifted off to sleep.

THE SOUND OF A RUMBLING truck coming up the pass caught Khloe's attention. She'd been up since the sun broke through the canopy and flooded the room with bright light. Unable to sleep, she started the coffee and went to the patio with a bowl to harvest berries. Not wanting to wake her husband, brushing her teeth would have to wait, or she would need to bring her toothbrush into the water closet if she was spending more time on the couch.

Her back said she wasn't and tonight she would sleep in that bed with him, whether he was comfortable with it or not. If push came to shove, they could line the middle of the bed with pillows, but she wasn't spending another night on the couch. Gathering the bed coverings, she stuffed them under the credenza just in case his brother wanted to come inside.

Plucking an avocado from the tree, she made a quick butter from the fleshy contents and spread it over toast with a poached egg. She poured a cup of coffee into a travel mug and had it ready for him when he walked out of the bedroom.

"Morning, Wife," Beau said, carrying his boots.

"Good day to you, husband," she said. "I made you a power breakfast; didn't want to start the blender with you still sleeping."

"Thank you very much," he said, watching her put the saucer on the counter, seeing the egg seated center over green stuff. "What is it?"

"A poached egg on toast with an avocado butter," she said proudly.

"That sounds nasty as hell," he chided.

"Says the man who ate two servings of chopped up pig shitters," she said, coming around to hand him his coffee. Khloe leaned down for a kiss with coffee breath laced with strawberries. He returned the kiss as his brother tapped on the glass like a child in a candy store window. Beau waved him inside.

"Let's go make this money, Bro," Lil Bo said. "Morning, Black Lady."

"My name is Khloe," she corrected.

"Yeah, and my name is Sherman Beauregard Montgomery," Lil Bo said.

"What?" Khloe responded, not understanding how two men had the same name in reverse order.

"We're twins," Beau said. "Ma and Pa had prepared to have only one, so they only had one name on the ready. Ten minutes after he was born, I surprised them and popped out. Hence the names."

"You said you were born ten minutes later, but he is called Lil Beau," she said.

"I'm bigger, he's smaller," Beau said. "And he is L.I.L. B.O., Lil Bo. I am B.E.A.U."

"Well, that clears up that," she said, passing a second container of coffee to his brother.

Lil Bo gave her a crooked, missing stained teeth grin, "He must not have done too much damage last night. You are up and able to move your arms and legs."

Beau was on his feet and in his brother's face. He had him by the front of his shirt lifting him off the floor. No words were spoken as he stared his brother in the eye then set him back on the floor on his feet.

"Sorry, Ms. Khloe, for disrespecting you in that way," Lil Bo said. "Won't happen again."

"Enjoy your day, gentleman," she said, not knowing how to react to her husband taking such a strong hand with his brother. She could count the number of times men who served beside her or under her leadership in the Army had stepped up and come to her defense. Usually, it was up to her alone to check them where they stood.

"Wife, come kiss me like you miss me," Beau ordered, but in front of his brother, she wouldn't give him a hard time for being high handed with her again.

She walked to him, yanking on his belt buckle. The twinkle in her eye brought a curve to his lips as her arms came around his neck, the long fingers entwining is his hair, also pulling playfully as she kissed him, full, hard, and with loads of tongue play. Letting him go, she moved to the kitchen to begin her own breakfast, leaving her husband to stand next to his brother, both with their mouths wide open as if to catch flies.

"Lil' Bo, I'm calling in sick today," Beau said, running his finger across his lips.

"Me too," Lil Bo replied, "I going to stay here with you and watch."

"Out, both of you. I have loads to get done today," she said, shooing them with her hands. "Hubby, you coming home for lunch, or do you want me to meet you at the office?"

"No, piddle around the house today, figure out what touches you want to add, work the garden, and get acclimated," he told her. "The air's not too thin up here, but coming from Chicago, you gone need a few days."

She gave him a mock salute as Lil Bo physically pulled him out the door. Beau didn't want to leave her alone, but he had work to get done. The school needed wiring. He also needed the check to pay for the honeymoon his wife deserved.

Beau saluted back, ever more reluctant to leave.

KHLOE STOOD ALONE IN the hexa-house, with loads to get done. Taking out her planner, she flipped open to the dates ahead, taking a gander at the month of September. All the little white boxes were blank with the exception of one sticker for Labor Day. She sat at the table, sipping on a mint, avocado, and strawberry smoothie and making a list of all the things she needed to get done.

- Weed garden
- Clean and sort the vegetables

- Check the jars for canning
- Put away the china
- Make dinner

"Shit, that's enough for one day," she said aloud, looking up at the sound of birds taking flight. Thinking they had been spooked, she got to her feet, moving to the kitchen window. Half-hidden behind the indoor edible garden, she spotted the top of what looked like a hat attached to a human head. It was moving. Coming down the hill through the wood line, entering the open patch of land just before the house. A man.

"Shit. Shit, Shit," she said, dropping to her knees and crawling to the cabinet which held the weapons. Taking out the rifle, she loaded in the clip, along with grabbing the 9mm and a Bowie knife, just in case things got close up and sticky. Dragging the items back to the kitchen in a modified low crawl, she rose slowly, peering through the hanging greenery to see if the man was still there.

"Where did he go?" she wondered, leaning over the counter. The rush of blood into her ears drowned out any thoughts other than stand and fight. Holding the 9mm low to her side, she moved to the sliding door to get a better look and spotted him standing below the steps. He just stood there as if he were waiting for her to see him.

Khloe moved forward, opening the glass door, flashing the metal of the weapon in the sunlight. The large gentleman removed his mountain man hat, looking up at her with hazel eyes, the top of his hair gray, graduating into the same strawberry blond hair of her husband. He also had the same nose.

The man pointed at the steps. Khloe nodded her head, going back inside to get two cups of coffee. She poured a little for herself and a whole cup for the man. On top of his cup, she set a saucer with one of Honey's biscuits, a smattering of jam and butter, and short handled butter knife. Stopping at her list on the table, she made a note to pick up a set of spreader knives. Holding both cups of coffee, she waited to see where he would choose to sit and make his introductions.

Walking across the open deck, he opened the door of the screened-in porch, found himself a seat and removed his hat. He sat there watching Khloe with bored interest waiting for her to join him. Opening the glass door first, then picking up the coffees, she handed the one with the biscuit and jam to him, the other she kept for herself as she took a seat across from the burly man.

As he drank the coffee and ate the biscuit, he didn't register as a threat to her, after she'd realized the mistake of leaving the weapon laying on the kitchen counter. They drank in silence, and she noticed the bandage on his hand. The cup empty and biscuit gone, he stared at her.

"Let me get my nursing bag, Mr. Montgomery," she said. "There's more coffee if you want it. Help yourself."

Erica's old nursing school bag still came in handy in her Mother's neighborhood back home. The modern term they used for the new graduates was a community nurse bag which her mother always kept fully stocked in case of emergencies for gunshots, cuts, and bruises. Before leaving Chicago, she'd restocked it with fresh supplies and brought it outside to care for her new patient.

"Hold your hand out for me, sir," she said, putting on a pair of gloves and peeling off the dirty bandage. The man had nearly severed his index finger off with a long ugly cut across the flesh, which she pulled back to see the exposed bone. "This could turn ugly, but I think you got here in time."

Khloe worked, explaining what she was doing as she went along. "First I need to assess how deep this cut is and whether or not it will require stitches," she said, even though she already knew it did.

"This is a deep cut," she said to the wound. "Let's get this cleaned out, so I can take a better look."

A small bowl was removed from the blue bag along with a small bottle of sterile water. Holding his hand over the bowl, she rinsed, inspected, and rinsed again. From the bag, she removed what looked like a baby diaper and lay his cleaned hand upon it, face up.

"Next, we are going to apply an antibiotic ointment, then I will need to sew it up," she said. "Let me know if you want me to give you a couple of pokes with the needle to numb the area."

For the first time, he spoke. "Can't hurt no worse than it already do," he said. "Just sew it up."

Khloe worked quickly and efficiently stitching the broken skin together and applying a bandage first around the finger then the hand. She provided him with a breathable safety glove to cover the bandaging. "Keeping your hand dry will be important to the healing of the wound and to avoid infection," she said to Mr. Montgomery.

He opened and closed his fist a few times, but the movement was limited.

"If it's too tight, let me know and I can loosen it up a bit," she said.

"Naw, it's okay," he said, watching her again with old eyes that had seen a great deal. Khloe put her things away as he sat looking about. "Don't keep no money on me, but in payment, I can help you weed that garden. Two of us can get it done in no time."

"You sure you want to do that with a sore hand?"

"It only takes one hand to pull weeds," he said.

"Thanks, I would appreciate the help," she replied, getting to her feet.

"You need on boots. Got any?"

"Yessir," she said.

"Long sleeves, too," he said, putting the hat back on his head and walking through the screened door. "Get changed. Meet you there."

Now she understood where her husband got his high-handed manners. However, she wasn't one to argue with a gift horse who offered to haul the load of firewood. Making quick work of her clothing change, she exited the sliding glass bedroom doors, walking at a clip to meet him in the garden. An hour later, they were done. He even killed a snake while they were working and to her joy, he took the dead carcass with him.

"Makes great stew," he said.

"I'll just take your word for that," she said with wide eyes.

The old man smiled. His teeth weren't in good shape, slightly yellowed and few broken. He nodded his head as he stuffed the decapitated snake into his bag, then asked for a cabbage that he also placed in the bag, before heading over the rise to the steps.

"If you ain't got no plans, you and my boy come up for supper this weekend," he said. "I'll have Ma cook you up a meal a city gal would like."

"By that, you mean no possum pie or rattlesnake stew? Thanks, my citified sensibilities appreciate you," she said.

He smiled again at her, this time wider. "Albus," he said, "or you can call me Pap or Pa, whichever rolls out smoother across your citified sensibilities."

"Khloe or Woman, as your son likes to call me," she told him. "That whole woman thing doesn't sit well with me, though."

"Or your citified sensibilities?" he said with a wider grin. "In these parts, Beau using that word means a great deal. Not like a possession, but a label for the one he has chosen to be his. No man dares cross him or touch *his woman*. You shall be cared for and looked after even if his eyes closed tomorrow. His folks are now your folks."

It happened. Just when she thought it never would occur until the first born she'd created slipped out of her baby maker that she would find a reason to smile, Albus Montgomery made her lips move into a semi half-moon.

"Pap, that means a lot, especially hearing it come from you," she said.

He raised his gloved hand, mumbled thanks, and set out back up the hill from whence he came. An odd odor wafted up, hitting her in the nose. Sniffing about to find the smell, Khloe realized with some dismay, that the scent was her own body. She smelled like a rat had climbed into her trousers and died. The long ride, the wedding, and sleeping on a couch bed without any water touching her body had left its mark. Heading to the bathroom, Khloe noticed that the bathroom door locked but no others in the house did.

Securing herself inside the bathroom, she showered and changed into a loosely fitted dress. As she pulled the fabric over her head, her stomach rumbled, indicating her body required food. Coming from the bedroom into the main house, she screamed at the back of a man's head sitting at the kitchen table.

Jethro screamed, too.

"What the hell is wrong with you screaming like that? You scared the bejeezus out of me," he said.

"Why in the hell are you sitting in my kitchen?"

"I brought you lunch and a cell phone," he said.

"I have a cell phone," she countered.

"It won't work up here, you have to have a phone that uses Montgomery Communications chip," he said. "Beau's company is the only provider in a 50-mile radius."

"Then put the chip in my phone," she snapped at him.

"Didn't think about that," Jethro replied, looking down at his hands and the gift he'd brought, feeling hurt by her dismissal. Khloe read the feelings of rejection off his expression and tempered her tone when she spoke to him again.

"Mr. Montgomery, Magistrate, Jebbo, I'm sorry. You gave me a fright," she said. "My apologies, and thank you for bringing me lunch."

"Jethro, my name is Jethro and well, that's more like it," he told her, feeling more satisfied in the change in her tone. "I would have called, but I didn't have your number. Even if I did, the Community Nurse needs to be a local number for the business and such."

"So, this is an official visit," she said.

"Kinda," he replied, his cheeks growing warm under her scrutiny. "Figured you might have been lonely and scared up here, so I brought lunch and wanted to tell you about Friday movie nights at my place. Me and Ennis love the old Hollywood movies, cowboys, murder mystery, dramas, and such."

"That is so sweet of you," she said, taking a seat at the table and looking at the salads Jethro had brought. "Oh, these look good."

"I enjoy a good salad at lunchtime over a piece of fried pork for dinner," he said. "I swear Ennis thinks everything has to be deep fried or simmered in pork fat to be tasty."

"I kind of prefer duck fat personally," she told him, opening the salad.

"A woman after my own heart," he said, smiling at her. "Your picture didn't do you justice. You are right pretty."

"Second time I've heard that," she replied, squinting her eyes at him.

"It's true. Eat up, I have to get back to work, and we have a lot to cover between now and Monday," he said. "You will get a part-time assistant, and she ain't that bright, but a tad bit of help is better than none at all. I scheduled the kids by ages for shots starting on Tuesday. That way by the end of the week, the crying will be over and just bigger kids being surly."

Khloe eyed the schedule and pushed it to the side, focusing instead on the company and Jethro's offer of friendship. She dug deep into his relationship with Ennis, whom he spoke of frequently in his discourse, which Khloe appreciated in an effort to obtain an understanding of the man. The gratitude with his help was welcomed and needed.

"I look forward to repaying the favor," she said.

"Anytime you are free to join me for lunch will be payment enough," he said. "Just a bit of fresh conversation is like a Godsend to my ears."

Jethro left a copy of the dense schedule but cautioned that it would change frequently between today and Monday and not to set her goals too high. The only real goal she tried to set was getting her items put away before her husband came home, which didn't seem to be happening any time soon. Especially after the departure of Jethro and the arrival of Katy Mae in a swimsuit with one jar of dark-colored moonshine that looked more like apple juice and one that was clear as water.

"Hey Girl, it's hot tub and mountain margarita time," Katy Mae shouted into the glass door.

"Mountain margaritas?"

"Hell yeah, margaritas made with moonshine versus tequila. This jar has been aged a week. The darker jar I've had since I was a kid. Two drops of this and you'll come out the bathroom with your panties on sideways," Katy May said, turning on the jets for the hot tub. "Come on, Sister Girl, join me."

"Do I need to get the blender?"

"Frozen margaritas are for fancy bitches," Katy Mae said turning on the hot tub jets. "I just need to burn off some brain cells before having to go back and deal with them damned kids."

"Katy, you work in the school system?"

"Yeah, I teach 6th grade Social Studies," she said. "And It's Katherine Mae. Honey Montgomery gave her sons the same damned name and me two that is pronounced as one, that she conveniently condensed to Katy Mae. Go figure."

Khloe watched her sister-in-law remove the oversized shirt and climb into the hot tub. She sighed like a lover had just touched her special place as she lowered her bottom into the water, the hefty boobs bobbing in the bubbles as she reached for the travel cooler, the moonshine, and a can of Squirt.

"Let me change into a suit and join you," Khloe said, forgetting about the things she said she'd get done today.

"Great, I even brought a surprise," Katy Mae said, holding up a small bag of quickly melting ice. "I scored us some ice cubes for our drinks. Bring back some glasses."

"Katy Mae, I'm not a drinker," she said. "But I will have one with you."

"Me neither, but I can't drink with just anybody. Most of these folks I'm either related to or teach their kids, so having a real friend that doesn't have skin in the game is a life changer for me," Katy Mae told her. "I hope we can be friends. I could sure use one."

It began as two women in a hot tub having an afternoon drink. Beauregard returned home later that evening to find his wife laid out on the bed with both long chocolatey legs through one leg hole of her panties and his drunk sister, who evidently gave up trying to put hers on at all. Katy Mae's panties lay in the floor, the crotch facing up and the two leg holes stretched open wide at her failed attempts to marry the holes to her feet. She lay on the bed like a toddler, her butt stuck up in the air as drool oozed from her open mouth onto his pillow. Growling, her threw a blanket over her girly parts and kicked the panties to the side near her shoes. He didn't even want to know why they were off as he went looking for an additional light blanket to cover his wife.

"Glad they got along so well," he said, going to the kitchen to start himself a bit of dinner. The good news was that the kitchen island was loaded with fresh-picked and washed fruit, which meant she actually got around to weeding the garden. The takeout trays of salad in the trash along with the Montgomery Communications phone box indicated Jethro had also been to the house. Looking deeper into the trash, he spotted the dirty rag with an old blood smudge. "Pap's been here, too."

He went back to the bedroom and threw the light coverlet on the other half of the Danger Sisters and sat down in front of his television with a sandwich, a semi-cool beer, and a huge grin on his face. His wife must have had a hell of a day, with visits from his Pa, Sis and Jethro. Beau's concerns about his woman being lonely were abated.

Khloe was getting along just fine.

Chapter Ten – Bottoms Up.

Khloe woke up, groggy, completely inebriated, smelling sour and rolled over into a solid mass. Pushing at the unmovable mass, trying to force it out her way proved futile as her head swam and the words inside of her skull jumbled together. She tried sitting up but the sharp pains shooting across her forehead made her lie back down. It helped very little to have the bright rays of morning light shining on her face like a cop doing a late-night search in a back alley. She groaned loudly, letting out a large gust of moonshine fueled air which, if she had been near an open flame, would have ignited the whole house.

"I see you are awake," a deep voice said.

Unfocused eyes tried to zoom in on the voice, but the blurry vision in her right eye prevented her from seeing anything clearly. Her hand reached out, patting, feeling its way toward the sound and came in contact with a hairy arm but she continued patting her way to the sound of the voice. Khloe jumped when her hand reached a wet hair-covered mouth. The throb in her head slowed her actions from getting away from the furry faced loud speaker.

"What are you doing in my couch bed?" she slurred.

"We are not on the couch, but in the bed," the voice replied.

"Oh shit," she said. "Did you try anything with me? My husband is going to be so mad if you did. He's gone kick yo' ass for touching me."

The booming voice said, sounding slightly amused, "Really?"

"Yeah, he's a big mufucka, too," she said, gripping the covers. "I've been trying to sneak and feel him up and see if he has a big mufuckin' pee-pee, but he keeps avoiding me. Saying he wants to wait for us to be friends, but I think he's just scared."

"Scared of what, might I ask," Beau said to her.

"You know what they say, once you go Black...," Khloe started to say but became distracted by the tangle of covers around her legs. It was all too much to process. The drumming of blood rushing to her ears, the loud voice talking to her, the big man in her bed, and the damned covers holding her hostage forced a low growl from her mouth in frustration.

Beau knew she was still drunk as was his sister who slept it off on the couch. That old bottle of moonshine she'd kept since she was 13 years old was a menace. His wife was the latest victim of the brown bottle of bothersome.

"Khloe, what do they say happens when you go Black," he asked, turning to his side to face her.

"Your credit gets fucked up," she said, giggling, her hands going to her face. "Oh shit, I'm laughing. I am actually smiling. Feel my face. It's a smile."

"A lovely smile it is," he said with his hand coming up and caressing her cheek.

"Don't get too familiar there, buddy! I'm a married woman and my husband is one big mufucka!"

"As you've mentioned," he said, helping her with the covers she struggled to untangle from her legs. Finally, free she looked down at her body, cross-eyed style and gasped.

"Whus' my panties?" she asked him. "Did you violate me? Oh shit, you're in trouble now! My husband is going to kick your ass and he can, too, you know why?"

"Because he's a big mufucka?"

"Yep," she said, stretching her legs open, sticking her hands between her thighs. "It's dry down there and not sore, so I guess you didn't stick anything in Pooh's honeypot!"

"Khloe, you are still drunk," Beau told her, trying not to laugh.

"Why in the *twitty tister* would I be drunk? I don't drink to get drunk, not even soberly," she said. "My Mama was a drunk. Burned down my house and everything in it. That's why I never take a drink to get drunk, me, my damned self, personally. Nasty habit. Not because I'm going to burn shit down, but because my Mama was a drunk. People act all crazy and shit when they drink. Tell all their damned business and yours, too!"

Beau lifted himself up on one elbow to look at his wife.

"*Twisty twitty*," she said. "No that's not right...*twibby tisty*." Then burst out in uproarious laughter.

"Your mother burned down your house, Khloe?" he asked, touching a strand of the wayward curl sticking straight up on her head.

"My Mama was crazy," she confessed. "Burned down my house and herself in it. She left me her house, though, and years of pissy, mildewed carpet. She also left me a brother who doesn't talk to me much and we're like strangers, but hey...hey...have you seen my panties?"

"They're in the laundry hamper," he said.

"Whoa, there's a laundry hamper. Whassit hamping?" she said, laughing. "Hey! Hey! You need to get out of here. I have to go make my huzzzzband some dinner. If not, he's gone come into this hexagon house and start yelling, 'Where's my food, woman!' He likes to call me that. All Neanderthal and shit. Makes my nipples tingle."

She began to giggle again, this time holding her nipples. Beau pressed his lips together to keep from laughing. He fully knew this was wholly unfair, but when life hands a man a lemon, might as well squeeze the hell out of them to get all the juice. This was juicy. His wife was actually open, not guarded like she usually was when they talked.

"I take it you like your husband?"

"Yeah, but he's a big mufucka," she said with her eyes wide, blinking as she tried to focus on his face. "I know I'm gonna have be on top when we finally get around to doing the loving. If I'm on the bottom, shiiiiit, you may find me in here still stuck to the mattress with my pelvis snapped in two. I'd die happy, too. I haven't had a good fuck in so long, my shit gets wet every time it hears a buzzing sound. I had to take my phone off vibrate 'cause my kitty thought it was date night errytime a bitch got a phone call."

Beau started laughing.

"That shit ain't funny. Men know women like sex too, but me, I'm gonna put it on that big mofucka so good, he's gone buy me anything I ever wanted," she said. "Hey guess, what? *Maty Kae* brought us a bag of ice, but she dropped it in the hot tub, then it was just a bag of cool water. I told her that my husband would buy me an ice truck if I asked him."

His eyes got wide, "Is that what you need from your husband, Khloe? For him to buy you everything you ever wanted?"

"He can't buy me a family who loves me," she whispered. "That's all I've ever wanted."

"What about other things in life that you want?"

"Like what – some panties? I could sure use a pair of those instead of layin' here with my honeypot all exposed. I'm telling you, if my husband comes in here and sees us like this, you are in trouble," she said, touching his chest, her eyes trying to open wider. "Whoa, you're a big mufucka, too."

She looked like a chocolate angel baby doll, lying on the bed, all exposed and vulnerable. Insecurity made him ask the next two questions, but he needed to get a better understanding of why she was here. Why she agreed to be his wife. Beau also wanted a clear direction of her heartfelt desire in order to make her continue the laughter and her smile.

"Khloe, why did you marry him, if you don't mind me asking?" Beau said.

"The same reason he married me," she said, the need for sleep taking her over the ability to think clearly. "Nobody wants to really be alone in the world. At the end of the night, you want to come home to another person who thinks you're cool as fuck and they are happy to see you. Nerd. Idiot. Drooling maggot, don't matter none to the person in your house. There is a nerdy, drooling idiot maggot waiting at home when you get there."

"All happy as fuck to see you," he said.

"Exacta *twitty tister*," she said, grinning. "I think you fixed my face. It can't stop making that weird thing that happens when my lips pull back and expose my teeth... Hey! Have you seen my panties? I know I need to buy some more. Did I tell you my Mama burned down my house? She burned up my panties, too. Left a bitch with two pairs of drawers. I bought a pack but I had to travel light."

"Khloe, I think you need some water," he said, going to the bathroom to fill a glass. Returning with a glass in hand, reaching the side of the bed, helping her sit upright so she could drink. The bed gave under his weight as he took a seat next to her, raising her head to sip at the water. "Slowly. Slowly."

"Thank you," she told him. "I seem to be saying that a lot. There are really nice people here."

Beau posed his final question, "If there was one thing you could ask your husband to give you, what would that be?"

"Fairness," she mumbled. "Like now, it's not fair that I laid down on this bed and when I woke up it was a whole 'nother day. That shit just ain't fair. I was 'spose to make my man a nice meal, but instead, I'm in here with no drawers on talking to a dude who may be trying to violate me for all I know."

"Help me out, Khloe, how can your husband give you fairness?" Beau asked.

"Easy," she said, leaning into the pillow and taking his fingers. "Every hand I have ever been dealt has been loaded with low cards of unfairness until it robbed me of my ability to smile. I only need him to show me that life has a good side as well. Will you tell him that when you see him? Tell my husband I just want him to be fair."

She fell asleep holding onto his hand, a soft touch which melted the hardened barriers around his heart. Fairness was all she wanted from him. He could give her that and so much more.

KATY MAE STOOD IN THE kitchen next to her big brother sipping on a strong black cup of coffee, staring out the window. She knew her brother would be furious with her for getting his wife slap up-side the head drunk, but she didn't know the woman was a featherweight when it came to liquor. It had been a great deal of fun, but that wasn't her brother's type of entertainment.

"Morning," he mumbled, pouring himself a cup of coffee. "Katy Mae, how much did she have to drink yesterday?"

She picked up a shot glass and showed it to him.

"You're telling me she had a whole shot glass of that stuff to drink?" he asked in disbelief.

"No, she had a teaspoon of my good stuff in this glass that was filled the rest of the way with Squirt," she told her brother. "You know she told me she didn't really drink, but I've heard that before. Remember Sally Jean? She said she didn't drink and downed half a gallon of Pa's corn mash."

"A teaspoon and she is down like that?"

"Beau, I think this may be the best sleep she's had in years. Did you know she's traveled the world?"

"Oh yeah?" He said, surprised at that bit of information, he kind of knew, considering she'd been in the Army, but he hadn't had an opportunity to discuss all the places she'd been stationed.

Katy Mae was pleased as punch to fill him in, telling her brother, "She went to the Olympics in Brazil, traveled to Cape Horn, and even Australia!"

"You sound like you want to date the woman," Beau said facetiously.

"No, it's just nice to a have another lady to have a conversation with that can actually add real and interesting points on topics with facts," Katy Mae said. "I would love to have her come to my Social Studies class as a guest speaker. It's too bad all the pretty treasures she collected from all over the world got burned up in the house fire. You know her Mama burned down her house? Herself in it!"

"Yes, I know," he said, raising the mug to his mouth, but stopping midway at the sight of his father coming across the back deck. "What in the hell?"

Katy Mae turned around to see their father taking a seat on the deck like he was waiting for the waitress of the establishment to come and take his order. She poured her Pap a cup of Joe and took it out to him. Beau followed along behind her addressing his father first.

"Morning, Pa," he said. "Everything going okay?"

Feeling guilty for showing up unannounced, Albus raised his arm to show the dirty dressing on his hand. "I got it dirty," he said, looking away like a child in trouble.

"Khloe is not feeling well today. Pa you need me to rewrap that for you?" Beau asked.

"Hell no," he said, grumbling. "I came to have my coffee with my daughter-in-law and get a new dressing for my wound. Damn near cut off my finger, but she sewed me up real nice like yesterday. What's wrong with her? You over-sexing that sweet young woman, you big galoot?"

"Pa! No," Beau said. "Katy Mae brought that brown jar of poison over here for drinks and the poor thing has been out since yesterday."

"Anybody made her a get better drink?" Albus wanted to know.

"I think it's best if we just allow my wife to sleep it off," he told them both, his attention now drawn to a vehicle coming up the pass. It was Jethro. "What in the hell does he want this early in the morning?"

Albus drank his coffee as he looked at the dressing he'd intentionally gotten dirty so he could have Khloe put on a fresh one. It defeated the purpose to have his son do it. If that was the case, he could have let Honey put on a new dressing, which she offered to do, but he wanted to talk a bit more to the woman who'd married his son. Now his nephew was coming as well, the interlopers irritating the old man, breaking in on his time with Khloe.

Jethro climbed the steps as everyone went to greet him. He issued a good morning to all his family and gave a sly grin to Beau. Normally at this time of the day, his cousin would have been at work. "Hey, why is everyone here? Is Khloe okay?"

"She's a bit under the weather this morning," Beau offered.

Jethro hit him with the back of his hand like a boy acting out in Sunday school. "You went at her too hard, didn't you? Poor thing, having to lay under all that bear meat and act like she likes it. Where is she? I would call a doctor but she is the only medical professional in these parts for 100 miles and you broke her!" Jethro yelled.

"I didn't break her, and why are you at my home when I would normally be at work Jethro?" He asked. "You making moves on my woman?"

"No, of course not," he said. "I was going to see if she wanted to get out of the house today and maybe go for a drive, you know to pick up things she may need."

"That is for her husband to take care of, boy," Albus said. "Get to work all of you."

"I'm staying to see about her while you're at work, Beau," Katy Mae said. "Pa, let me make you a bit to eat."

"Your Ma fed me already. I just came to have my bandage changed and have coffee," he said, hiding his hand he'd stuck in the dirt on his way down the mountain.

"Jesus, walk with me," Beau said wiping his hand across his eyes. "Two days. I have been married for two days and you all have turned my life upside down. I have to go. Please, Katy Mae, call me if she...if my wife needs anything. You all do realize this is nuts!"

"No, what's nuts is that you said please," Katy Mae said. "I love her already."

KHLOE LAY QUIETLY IN bed listening to the Montgomery's fighting over her. To wake up in a home filled with people who cared for each other touched her expressive side, which she had tucked away in her emotional safe until the arrival of her future children. She fought back the tears threatening to blow the door off the safe and let all the stored-up tears come out and gush forth like the dam held together by one or two dikes. It was a good thing she held the tears as Beau's heavy footsteps could be heard coming into the bedroom. Khloe kept her eyes closed, pretending to be sleep as he adjusted the covers around the legs.

He'd slept beside her last night and didn't make a move to touch or be intimate. Based on the current state of her brain cells, she must have been drunk. In her Army days, a drunk woman in bed with you would be taken as consent. Even as his wife, he didn't take advantage. For that alone, he'd earned her respect.

"I've put a couple of headache tabs on the nightstand with a glass of water. Sleep as long as you need to and Katy Mae is going to spend the day with you until I get home," he said. "Pap dirtied his bandage to come back to have coffee with you this morning. Of course, Jethro showed up to take you for a morning ride."

Strong fingers ran down the side of her face. Taking a moment to rest on the soft cheek, loving the feel of warm, dark flesh under the tip of his finger. He felt the dampness on her skin, wiping away the wetness.

"It seems as if your wishes are coming true, little lady, although I'm not sure which one you want to label as the drooling maggot, but they must all think you are cool as fuck," he told her. "Sleep it off, and we will start our weekend when I get home."

A feathery light kiss went to her forehead. The warmth of his hand nested inside the limp one on the bed. Khloe fingers closed over his hand, giving a slight squeeze. Beau didn't think now was the time to address the tears and left her alone to process the emotions flooding through her.

He needed to deal with his own as well. His wife was indeed a formidable lady and he was one drooling maggot who couldn't wait to get home to hang out with the woman. In his eyes, she was cool as fuck.

Chapter Eleven – The Past is a Present

The hour was well after five when Khloe began to feel human and rolled her aching body out of the bed to take a shower. She washed from her head to down between her toes and everything in between at least twice. The stench of aged moonshine in her pores permeated her nose like an offensive body lacking access to water and soap. Finally satisfied and remembering Beau's warning about making the showers brief, she exited the shower, toweling dry and putting on a light sleeveless sundress with a matching mini cardigan. The evenings had begun to cool considerably in the last few days and a shopping trip would be required sooner rather than later.

Entering the main living space, Khloe spotted Beau bending over the stove, taking a pan of biscuits out of the oven. Remaining quiet, just watching him in the kitchen prepare a meal for the two of them, made her feel some kind of way. Gently, he cut the tomatoes, carrots, and cucumbers for a green salad. Moving from the island to the stove, he stirred a pot of what she assumed, based on the smell, was a stew.

"Whatever it is, it smells heavenly and I could eat a horse at this point," she said, walking all the way into the kitchen to greet her man. On her tiptoes, she leaned upward to kiss his cheek, but he turned his face, his lips briefly meeting hers, sending sparks down her spine.

"I was about to come and wake you, but then I heard the shower," he said. "Dinner is almost done. Will you please set the table?"

"Dinner. Certainly," she said absently collecting two of the four plates he owned, as well as two of the four forks. "I am grabbing spoons as well. Beau, did I hear people here today?"

"That was yesterday. You have been asleep for nearly two days," he said, pointing at the two-salad bowls he possessed. "Katy Mae said you only had a teaspoon full of that brown brain buster of hers."

"Katy Mae didn't bother to mention how many teaspoons she gave me," Khloe said. "I'm not a drinker, you know. Erica, my mother, was an alcoholic, which makes me only have an occasional drink to steady my nerves. Drinking to get hammered, I avoid like the plague. Drinking something a fermented as that moonshine was a dumb thing to do, but man, is your sister a lot of fun, even sober."

"Well, that shit has fermented alright," he said. "Moonshine is not brown. You and Katy Mae had a bonding moment through the experience. She's been longing for a friend. So, tag, you're it."

"I guess we're bound to be friends after you help a woman use the toilet and wipe her honeypot," she said, finding the desire to want to smile.

"Honeypot?"

"Erica was an OB nurse. She looked at vaginas all day and referred to them as honeypots," Khloe said, taking a seat at the table. "It was dinner conversation after work. 'That girl's honeypot has seen too many bees. That honeypot has fermented and turned sour'. Those kinds of weirds conversations stuck with me, so I ended up calling it a honeypot as well."

"Only if it tastes sweet," he said, furrowing his brow. "Sorry, that just slipped out."

"As long as your tongue accidentally slips in," she said with a wink.

Beau brought the food to the table, uncovering the pot of thick, hearty stew. Khloe wanted to eat it, but after watching Pa Montgomery decapitate a rattler to take home for dinner; stew wasn't on the top of her list of things to eat, especially since she didn't see the shape and bones of the animal going into said pot.

"Relax, it's chicken gumbo," he said. "After dinner, I was thinking we could spend some time in the hot tub, maybe make out a little, let me find a few of those buttons to push."

"You only need to know where the main one is, rub it, push it, and kiss it," she said with her lips curling at the corners.

"Woman, you keep talking like that and the honeymoon is going to get real fun, real fast," he said, grinning at her. His eyes went to her breasts to see if he could, in fact, witness a reaction in her breasts to being called woman.

Khloe said nothing as she picked up one of the biscuits and ripped it apart. She shoved a corner of the breaded delight in her mouth, chewing slowly, wanting to counter his flirting but afraid of it going too far too fast. Years ago gave her a hardbound copy of *Eat That Frog*, a book on how to stop procrastinating. He was procrastinating on making love to her and she appreciated the attempt to create intimacy between them before making their connection be based mainly on sex. Her husband was a lot of frog; a plan of attack had to be figured out before trying to eat it.

With a Mona Lisa smile, they ate in silence, enjoying the company of sharing a meal, saying everything with no words at all.

THE TEMPERATURE OF the hot tub hovered just under perfect as cooler evening air swirled over Beau's sore shoulders and aching back from stooping, bending, and squatting while running fiber optic lines. The kids would be in the modern age but his back felt as if he'd been Hebrewing loads of mud and clay to build Pharaoh's temples. A cold beer in his hand was almost as satisfying as watching the long, dark legs step into the water to join him.

"Sit next to me, Wife."

"Not sure if I want to do that," she said. "I'm uncertain about your intentions."

"I intend to get to know you a little better, and you need to get to know me as well," he said. "How about we start with a kiss?"

"How about no?" she said to him, slapping the water. "Tell me, Beauregard Montgomery, you have a way with women, what made you place an ad for a mail order wife?"

"I don't have a way with women, I just have come across too many that are fragmented," he said. "A few by their own design, others by bad choices around immature men."

"Surely you can't believe that women are at fault for men being assholes and taking advantage of situations," she said, sitting closer than she'd planned. The water warmed her entire body until sweat beads started to roll down her back between the shoulder blades.

"There are circumstances, Khloe, that can be out of a woman's control, but there are times when the situations for victimization are created by the woman herself," he said, touching a wayward curl of her hair. His eyes, twinkling as his hand came out of the water, interlacing with her own.

"Explain yourself, husband," she said, squeezing the fingers intertwined in hers.

"When I was in college, at UT, there were always these frat parties. I can't tell you how many times a young lady would walk through the door and a random dude handed her a drink," he told her. "If you don't know the man, don't take the drink."

"That part I understand," she replied. "My first year in the Army was like a daily walk down a dick gauntlet. Every corn husker from any corner of the world thought I was easy pickings. A lot of the young women from small towns found themselves the subject of Monday morning gossip around the water cooler. Even when they were warned to conduct themselves properly in foreign countries, late at night the moans of passion could be heard crawling across the desert sands."

She touched the hairs on his chest, her fingers toying with the strands, sliding down the broad expanse of muscles, touching the belly button. Beau grabbed her hand before she could take it any lower.

"I need to know what makes you tick before I get too wrapped up in ticking you," he said.

"You are an odd man."

"No, I learned the hard way that eight out of ten women have been hurt in one form or another," he said. "I found a few that were obvious. You know the *easy* ones. Coming from a mountain community, we had access to the girls who would *let* you as well as the ones you knew not to touch, but you kinda did anyway. Yet, living in Knoxville for a couple of years, working for a Fortune 500, I came in contact with the other kind."

"The other kind?"

"Women who are beyond your reach and refuse to go get help. Those you find out about the hard way," he said. "Case in point: Laqueta. I found the darkness she hid her truth inside of one night after a football game. I came up behind her, all sexy like, to kiss her neck and bobble a boob, to be met with a butcher knife to my throat. Turns out her stepfather liked to do that to her as well."

"The way you speak, you talk as if there has been more than just one Laqueta," she said.

"Oh, don't get me started," he said. "Not that I was a man whore, but I am drawn to the broken-winged birds as if I can heal them and make them whole. Standing over your lady's bed at night, that's a no. A reach around for a little warm up, that's a hell no. So, I stopped dating."

It was the way he gazed at Khloe that said it was her turn to spill the beans. She obliged his inquiry by taking a quick jog down the memory of her past roads less traveled.

"My career came first, then saving the lives of soldiers," she confessed. "Most of the higher ranking or equivalent ranking officers were already married, or had girlfriends, or were married with girlfriends. I just didn't want to spend my evening with a man whom I worked with all day, talking Army talk."

"You did 20 years in the Army, correct?"

"Yes, 20 long years working with men with inflated egos and misogynistic views on women, and then, in my brilliance, I kind of dated a boy child who liked to travel the country playing poker," she said. "He dumped me on the same day I landed on Coraline's doorstep."

"And now you're on mine," he said, leaning forward to kiss her. "Living with you is going to be easy. I suspect that loving you won't be a hard thing to do either."

"Coming home each day to you is going to be nice as well," she said. "I think you are cool as fuck."

"I'm a big mufucka, too, with a gentle touch," he said with a grin. "I have a gift for you."

"I just bet you do."

"No seriously, here," he said, giving her the small box that rested behind his large body on the side of the hot tub. "Every Montgomery woman has one of these. At big family functions like the Autumn Equinox Festival, sisters, wives, first cousins all wear the crest. Allow me to place yours upon your neck."

Khloe opened the box and it was quite easily the most hideous thing she'd ever seen in her life. It looked like a red piece of leathery skin stretched over the missing tooth of a six-year-old with one eye. The one-eyed child was the base of the necklace with his face pressing through the red leather.

"Wow, look at that!" she said, thinking if she put it on, it would suck out her life force beginning with the marrow after it forcibly congealed the matter in her bones. Taking it in her hand, the family crest went back in the gift box.

"It's ugly, but a trademark. People will respond to you based upon that thing hanging around your neck. The response will be more favorable than not having it on," he told her.

"On Monday, I will wear it proudly," she said. "Tonight, hmm, no."

Beau stood up, making large tidal ripples in the water. Droplets splattered on her face and arms as he reached for her hand and yanked her to her feet. He said nothing as he headed for the bedroom, opening the sliding door after turning off the jets in the hot tub.

"I'm not sleeping on the couch tonight," she asked softly.

"Last two nights you've slept beside me. No need for tonight to be any different," he said, pulling her inside the hexa-house, and turning back the covers.

Chapter Twelve – Sssh! Sssh! ... Don't Shush Me!

Beau discovered very quickly that there was a gigantic difference between sleeping next to a woman who was damned near catatonic and having a live, wiggling, non-snoring one lying next to him, starting with those lips that begged to get kissed and a warm body that asked to be touched. Then she started touching him in all the right ways, giving him all the wrong ideas.

"Hey, Woman, stop that," he said. "You're making my body parts start to move."

"Good. Husband, I want to know what I'm going to be working with," she said, slipping her hands under the covers. Like a snake with its tongue out seeking warm prey, her hand slithered over his body, coming into to contact with his hairy thigh and finally the treasure she'd been wondering about for weeks. Reaching inside of his boxers, taking hold of him in her fisted hand, she squealed in delight. "Oooh, this is mine?"

"Technically, it's still mine," he said, swallowing hard at the sensations from the touch of her hand.

"But we are husband and wife," she told him, stroking gently up and down the shaft. "What's yours is mine and what's mine is yours."

The wonderful sensations ceased as she rolled to her back. Planting her feet firmly on the bed, she raised her hips to remove the underwear.

"Khloe, what are you doing?"

"We are going to play a little game, just like you did as a kid," she said, hiking up her gown and climbing on top of him.

He didn't want this. Not now. They still needed more time. He pushed at her shoulders, "Wait...wait, what are you doing?"

"You'll like it," she said, straddling his hips, the hardness of him nestled between her legs as she lowered her body on his. She sat atop him, the moisture covering the hardened muscle, her womanly lips seated perfectly over the rod, the nub enjoying the pressure. "Just a little dry humping between friends."

"Dry humping is done with your underwear on," he said, pushing at her hips, but the damned woman began to move against him, sliding back and forth. The heat. The moisture. The wanton, far off gaze on her face made him sigh in a self-imposed agony, wanting so much more. "You don't have on any."

"Ssh. Sssh," she told him as she slid her body back and forth. The friction of feeling him beneath her fueled her movements.

"Don't sssh me, Woman. Get off," he said, pushing at her shoulders, but she wouldn't budge.

"In a minute, I sure will," she said, leaning forward, increasing her pace.

"Khloe...," he started to speak, but she silenced him with her mouth, initiating a deep, lusty kiss with her tongue slipping inside of his mouth, playing, teasing, caressing his own. Beau moaned as she moved her hips faster.

"Damn, you sure are one big fella," she said, sitting upright, yanking her gown over her head.

The small breasts bobbed as she slid back and forth. His hardness jumped in anticipation of what was to come. He wanted to stop her. Beau also wanted to roll her over on her back and plant himself so deeply that when he finally came, her eyes would fill up with his love juices from her nose to her forehead.

This has to stop. Trying again, he raised his knees, to buck her off. "Khloe, please, we have to stop before we go too .... What in the fuck?"

Her finger was in his bunghole, probing around like she'd lost a ring. She kept pressing until she found what she'd been searching for and pressed down. Beau's hips came off the bed.

"Holy shit!" he called out, grabbing her hips, helping her slide back and forth. "Oh! My! Ggggghhhhhoooorrrdddd!"

"That's it, Big Daddy let go," she said as she began to grind against him faster, harder, as the nub came in contact with the tip of the erection. "Oh yeah, just like that."

Beau couldn't hold on. He whimpered as her finger pressed down against his prostate and he began to cum like a freight train on bad fuel; fast, hard, and sputtering almost out of control. His hands shook, his toes curled, and he howled like a banshee at a full moon.

Khloe collapsed on top of him, spent, sated, and thinking of what they could do the next time – especially how good it was going to be when he actually penetrated her.

"That was really stupid," he said, lifting her off of him, extricating her finger from his butt. "And you stuck your finger in my asshole!"

"Beau, there was nothing stupid about that. It felt good. You needed it and I sure as hell needed it as well," she said, standing up to go to the bathroom.

"Are you on birth control?"

"Hell of a time to ask," she said from the bathroom, turning on the taps at her vanity. She soaked a cloth, wiping away the remains of their lovemaking session. She felt energized and alive.

"Well, that should have been something we discussed before you decided to milk me like some stud bull," he said, getting to his feet on the other side of the bed. The wetness from their activity soaked the front of his boxers. His penis hung from between the slit in his drawers like a limp noodle coming out of the pool after a teenager's swim party. He made his way to the bathroom, moving inside to start the shower. "I wanted our first time to be special Khloe, not that. I don't even know what the fuck that was. I felt like I should have started humming or something."

"Sorry you are so disappointed in my need to spend an intimate evening with my husband," she said, rinsing the cloth and hanging it on the rack. His wife's nudity didn't seem to bother her, but it sure as hell was bothering him.

"That wasn't intimate. That was a tug and grab, and personally, I feel kinda used and dirty," he said, placing his hands over his nipples.

"Oh, for the love of Pete," she said. "You turn me on. I was turned on and needed some relief. I tried to find a happy medium and now you are acting like I took your virginity without your consent. I tell you what, I'll sleep on the couch until you're ready to share your bed."

"Stop it, Khloe! You are making me seem like some prude," Beau called after her.

"I was thinking you are acting more like a school girl who accidentally had an orgasm," she said, walking past him and yanking her nightgown and a pillow off the bed. "I'll be in my room on my couch bed. Goodnight, Mr. Montgomery."

"Woman! Stop and let's talk about this," he said.

"There's nothing to talk about. I was horny and took advantage of you. I'm sorry if I offended your delicate sensibilities," she said. "Honestly, I can't believe we are having this conversation. I seriously feel like I'm in an alternate universe."

"This could have been so different if you had just waited," he said softly.

"Well, this is what we have," she said, closing the bedroom door.

Beau showered and got into the bed which still smelled musky from her love. The coconut oil she used on her hair gently scented the pillow and the bed seemed empty without her there. Waiting was important to him. He had a plan.

The only problem was that Khloe didn't seem to give a shit about his plans.

BEAU AWOKE TO FIND the house empty. Making coffee and breakfast, he set the table, looking about for his wife. Calling out to her, he didn't receive an answer. Slipping on a pair of boots, he slid open the glass door and went out on the deck. Climbing over the small hill, he searched below in the garden. She wasn't there.

Panic filled him as he ran down past steps, looking for her car. It was gone. His heart thudded in his chest as he bolted up the stairs, searching the living room for a note. Finding none, he looked for his phone.

"Shit, where's my phone?"

Scrambling about the house, looking high and low, he made a beeline for his truck, hoping, praying that he'd left it connected to charge overnight. The phone wasn't in the truck. He sat in the vehicle, his forehead on the steering wheel, breathing deeply, praying for understanding on where she could have gone. Unable to find any reasonable solutions to a very vexing problem, he settled on the only answer he could come up with, "My wife has left me."

KHLOE LEFT THE NOTE taped to the mirror in the main bathroom. *Maybe I should have left it by the coffee pot. He'll see it*, she thought as she drove to Chattanooga to do a bit of shopping. It was only an hour and a half drive and she could be back before dinner. The house needed to be warmed up with her touches. Just to show people who popped in for coffee that she also lived there. Besides, she needed more plates, silverware, underwear, and towels. She'd purchased several packs but inadvertently packed them in the household goods she's put into storage. She found herself nearly smiling, thinking a nice piece of beef would be great for dinner as well.

The scenic drive gave her a sense of peace after the turbulent evening with Beau. She understood what he wanted and why he wanted it, but it didn't work for her and definitely didn't work for them. It may have been selfish on her part, but she needed comfort. *I lost my mother. My home. I have no one but him and Coraline. I needed my husband.*

"I should have respected his wishes," she said aloud. "I tried, but it's his own damned fault for putting me in that hot tub and being so big and sexy. Besides, he's my husband."

"YOU SCARED HER OFF, didn't you?" Jethro asked, sitting on the screened in deck, his legs crossed and mouth turned down. "Leave it to you. What happened, you couldn't have your way and went all caveman on the poor girl?"

"It was nothing like that, and just so you know, she went shopping," Beau countered. He didn't know where she was or if she would be coming back. Jethro saw the vehicle rolling through town and he couldn't resist riding up the mountain to see for himself that the Rubicon only had one head inside the vehicle. The one head was Khloe minus a Beau.

"Beau, I thought today you were spending time together, hiking, counting cabbage heads and putting them in jars," Jethro said.

"That's what I'm doing," he said. "She went to get more jars."

"The way she was driving, that woman looked like she was getting the hell out of Dodge. Beau, what did you do?" he asked again.

"Jethro, either you can come inside and help with the rest of the vegetables or you can go home," he said. "My marriage is just fine."

"Sure. Sure," he said, looking at his cousin with a side eye. "Where's your phone?"

"Charging," he lied.

"Charging where Beau?"

"For the love of God, would you please leave me alone? Go home. Pick eye of newt, make a potion of fairy dust, or give an old lady a ticket, whatever it is you do, just leave and go do it," Beau said to him.

"I'm not leaving you alone, Beauregard Montgomery," Jethro said, handing him the cell phone he'd left in his office. Sarah Jean had given it to Jethro to return to her boss over the weekend. "In times like these, a man needs his family around."

"There are no times like these," Beau said. "She has been cooped up here for days and wanted to get out and stretch her legs and flex her credit card arm. Please, just leave me alone so I can work."

"Fine," Jethro said. "But you can't say I wasn't here for you."

"I wish I could say you were anywhere else but here," Beau said, grabbing his cousin by the arm and escorting him to his vehicle. "Have a good day."

"Call me if you need me," Jethro said, climbing into his truck.

"I wouldn't call you if I did," Beau said, going inside to wash the dirt off his body. It was nearly five thirty. He turned on his phone, waiting for it to light up so he could check for messages and to see if she'd called.

She hadn't.

"Stupid. Stupid. Stupid," he said to himself as he started the taps. As he scrubbed his sweaty body, the sound of the water drowned out the rumbling of the wheels of the jeep as it climbed over the compacted soil and she parked. It took three times back and forth to the car before she unloaded all the touches she wanted to add to the hexa-house, starting with rugs and much-needed drapes. For all she knew, someone could be sitting on the deck in the dark looking into the bedroom. She shuddered as she grabbed the last load.

Darkness was coming earlier and earlier each evening. She didn't want it to catch her outside alone. Her cell phone rang as she entered the kitchen and unloaded the cooler with the steaks and shrimp. A rumbling stomach fueled her actions as she started dinner. The last thing she wanted tonight was more biscuits and stew.

"Hello," she said into the line.

"Khloe, this is Dr. Wells at Mercy General, how are you?" the voice said.

"I'm doing just fine, Dr. Wells. How may I help you?"

"I heard from Ms. Connors that you were getting married and had turned in your resignation," he said. "Is this true?"

"It's true. I'm married now and living in Tennessee," she said. "Is that why you called?"

"Dear, I called out of concern. I have always treated you like my daughter, and well, I feel poorly for not coming to your defense with Ms. Connors. You had just lost your mother, and I felt you needed time to grieve," Dr. Wells said.

"Erica was gone long before she died," Khloe told him. "Whatever ugliness happened to her went to the grave with her. I will never know the cause of her pain."

Dr. Wells asked with an air of suspicion, "Everyone has secrets, Ms. Burgess, or what is your new name?"

She didn't want to tell him. It wasn't his business. On top of the insult of calling her after she'd resigned, it was just too much. She had never liked the man, but he'd offered her the job when she returned to Chicago three years ago. He did, in fact, treat her like his daughter, giving her birthday presents, and even taking her to dinner on occasion. As much as she appreciated the call, he was part of her old life. Beau was the center of the new one.

"Dr. Wells, thank you for checking on me, but I'm fine, doing very well and enjoying my new life. I haven't seen a gunshot wound in three weeks. Life is good," she said. "Take care of yourself."

She hung up the phone and went back to seasoning the steaks.

"Where in the hell have you been?" a booming voice asked.

"Shopping," she said, almost giving him a smile. "Didn't you get my note?"

"What fucking note?"

"The one on the bathroom mirror," she said, going into the water closet and looking for the note. It had fallen to the floor behind the commode. "It fell behind the toilet. See, here it is. *Beau, went to Chattanooga, be back by dinner. Gone shopping.*"

"Woman, you didn't think to call your man just to touch base, let me know you were safe and not kidnapped by sex traffickers or worse?" He was still yelling although it wasn't his intention.

"I forgot to put the Montgomery Communications chip in my phone until I hit town and saw the big ass satellite dish," she said. "Why are you acting so grumpy and bossy?"

Beau didn't know whether to strangle the woman or kiss her. The sound of her voice in the house when the shower stopped nearly made his knees buckle.

He didn't even mind the mess of the bags all over the floor or the boxes she'd had yet to unpack. The place looked cluttered with junk that he didn't care to have laying about, and she was creating more trash with her bags and boxes. It only took six long strides to make it across the room and stand in front of her.

"I'm so sorry," he said taking her hand "I was thinking only of myself in asking you to wait. If my wife needs me to be her husband in every sense of the word, I'm yours, Khloe. I'm all yours."

She blinked several times, gawking up at him. "What has gotten into you, Beauregard Montgomery? You're acting all weird."

"I thought you'd left me," he said, placing his hands on her shoulders.

"And leave my mother's Wedgewood China? The hell you say," she said. "If the china is missing, then you know I'm gone. Wait...what?"

"Last night. Our fight," he said.

"That wasn't a fight. You were being dick stingy and I wasn't having it," she said. "I mean, I guess I kind of sexually assaulted you, didn't I? Sorry about that, but it's fault for being all big, and dangerous looking and sexy as hell."

Beauregard Montgomery was done talking. The only thing he planned to use his mouth for the rest of the night was to bring his wife pleasure. He left the steaks on the counter as he lifted her into his arms, carrying her to the bedroom for a long overdue wedding night.

"The steaks," she said.

"They can wait, I can't."

Chapter Thirteen – Easy Like...Sunday Morning

Beauregard Montgomery made love the same way he went through life, carefully, methodically, and with a plan. The rough brute Khloe expected to manhandle her in their bed was not the man she lay next to as they consummated the marriage. Slowly, item by item, he undressed her as well as himself, kissing, touching, and caressing her as he went along. He didn't seem to have the inclination to give her empty words of praise or bark commands to her while he warmed up her body for his entry.

Unhurriedly, he nestled close to her body, running calloused hands over the ebony skin, planting delightful kisses over her shoulders, neck, and breasts. Beau held her gaze when he connected their bodies, penetrating her leisurely as if he had all the time in the world. Adjusting their bodies to have her face him as they lay side by side, the angle of entry was just perfect enough to locate that one pleasurable spot on her insides Khloe never knew existed.

Beau didn't thrust or poke at her like a horny teenager in the back seat of a car but instead provided a consistent rhythm of rubbing a hardened sword over a smooth stone. Back and forth over the same perfect spot, creating a ripple effect in her body until, like a mother irritated by a child's constant tapping, her insides fisted, gripping the sword, holding on tight. A wave washed over her as Khloe's mouth opened, her head fell back, and fingers gripped his arms as she gave into the pleasure.

It didn't stop Beau's movements. He continued at the same rate. The same steady pace. The same rhythm until the second wave hit, making her whimper as his mouth found hers, kissing her with the same lazy ease while her toes curled, her pits sweated, and she clung to him for dear life.

Khloe's mouth was dry and she didn't think she could take any more. She begged him to join her, find his own pleasure, but he continued the slow torture.

"Not yet, Wife," he said softly. The slow rocking of his hips made the bed creak in protest, creating the only music they needed as the third wave started.

"Beau," she whispered, holding onto him as if he were the last buoy fallen over the side of a sinking ship. The tension she'd been holding in, the doubt, the uncertainty, she released and she wrapped her arms around the mass of man, planting kisses on his face and neck, crying out his name.

He joined her this time, and in the same gentle manner with which he started, her husband ended it the identical way. No fuss. No thrust. No loud nor boisterous cry of victory, but two strong hands, cupping her bottom as he finished with a heavy sigh. Her limp body lay wrapped in his large arms, the bear paw of a hand resting on her buttocks as he kissed the top of her head.

"You okay, Khloe?" he asked, his hand rubbing the firm flesh of her bottom.

"Yes, more than okay," she said, snuggling close, listening to the sound of his steady heartbeat. "That was beautiful."

"That's how it should be between a man and his wo...his wife," he corrected himself. "It's not about sex, but intimacy, and connection."

"We are definitely connected now," she said, feeling the start of a smile.

"As we always shall be," he told her, holding tighter, not wanting the moment to end. All day he had wrestled with himself and the mind-numbing fear that she had walked out on him, never to return. This moment would have never happened. This opportunity to show her how a man loves his woman versus jumping in bed and pounding her into submission would have been lost forever had she not returned. There was a time for those types of encounters, but the first one between a man and his wife, in his mind, needed to be a memorable experience of connection, not three humps and two pumps of aggression. He prayed she understood.

"Beau?"

"Yeah, Khloe?"

"It was worth the wait," she said. "I feel so...cherished," she told him, snuggling closer, inhaling the male scent of his skin.

"Because you are," he said, kissing her lightly on the lips.

"I like this feeling," she whispered, burrowing into the warmth of his arms. "I'm liking you more and more each day."

"I'm liking you too, woman."

THE EVENING WAS A QUIET one, as she cooked the shrimp, steaks and sautéed spinach for dinner. Beau offered to open a bottle of wine, which Khloe refused, opting instead to make a pitcher of tea, minus the ice. He held her hand and prayed over the meal, offering thanks for a tasty supper, cleaning his plate, leaving nothing on it but droplets of juice from the meat.

Together they washed the dishes and Khloe was ready to set to work on unpacking the bags and boxes to settle into her new home. It had been several days and it appeared that more clutter was accumulating than either she nor her husband was comfortable having around.

"Beau, where do I put the trash?" she asked, looking outside as if a magical dumpster would appear.

"I have to burn it, which is why we can the veggies in reusable jars," he said. "Some of the scrap and items that can break down go in the composter. We just have to remember to turn it once a week. I usually turn it on Sundays."

"So, I need to get this stuff put away and get our home in order. I'm sorry about the mess and clutter," she told him.

"Tomorrow," Beau said. "Tonight, is about me and you."

She didn't know what that meant, but her body wanted to get in the hot tub and soak away the dull ache in her hips from the round of easy loving which hit her lower back like a night of hard riding on an unfriendly horse.

"What do you have in mind?" she asked, feeling the unfamiliar twitch at the corners of her lips trying to make a smile.

"An easy evening, some music, talk about the books you brought, among other things," he said, standing in the middle of the floor like he was playing a game of Simon Says and waiting for the next command.

"Music, hey," she said, raising an arm and hitting her signature fancy move. Khloe thought the move was fancy. To Beau, it looked like a worm had fallen down her dress and she was wiggling trying to dislodge the creature.

"Uhmm, nothing like that," he said, frowning.

"Okay, then surprise me," she added, almost issuing him a challenge.

Beau surprised her in more ways than one. She discovered that night her husband could play the banjo. She also learned there was such an animal as jazz banjo, which confused and titillated her at the same time. Sitting on the couch with her feet tucked under her dress, she listened as he hit the chords, playing a song familiar to him that he'd loved since the first time he'd heard it. Billie Holiday, one of his favorite jazz artists, sang a song titled *Tenderly*, which was the first jazz song he'd learned to play.

"Tenderly," he sang softly, in a hillbilly drawl but with a jazz flair, as he plucked the strings of the black banjo. Lost in the words and the melody, he sang for her as if no one else in the world existed but the two of them. He strummed the chords with nimble fingers and finished the three-minute tribute, looking up from the instrument to his wife's face. He didn't know what to expect from her but he wanted to give her this personal gift from his heart.

Khloe was frozen, immobilized in her feelings by the sensual rendition of the Billie Holiday song she wasn't very familiar with, but her mother had played the artist on Friday nights in between her Millie Jackson and Betty Wright songs. *Jazz on a banjo. He can carry a tune. He played this for me.*

Then, the one thing he wanted more than anything in the world for his new marriage happened. Khloe Burgess Montgomery smiled at him. She showed her beautiful set of pearly whites, as the little crinkles formed at the edges of her eyes, and the smile widened.

"You're smiling," he said.

"You put it there," she responded, touching his thigh. "That was lovely."

'Thanks," he said, blushing. "Ready to call it a night?"

"After that, yes, I am," she said, getting to her feet.

She slipped her hand into his as they went back to the bed, facing the crumpled covers, still disheveled from their earlier lovemaking. Khloe changed quickly into a nightgown as Beau stripped down to his boxers. In the bed, she rested her hips into the crook of his body in a spooning position, cuddling up with him, holding onto his hand, pressing it to her heart. Beau's lips planted a light kiss on her shoulder, before drifting into a peaceful sleep.

This was the life he wanted.

This was the life he wanted with her.

This was the life.

KHLOE WOKE IN A TIZZY, wanting to get so many things completed before the evening came and she had to report to her new office in the morning. By the time Beau joined her in the kitchen, she'd eaten, had two cups of coffee, and unpacked three boxes. The china stood out in the formerly empty cabinet, giving the hexa-house a new ambiance as if people who lived inside mattered.

"Woman, slow down," he said to her.

"Beau, good morning. I have to get the boxes unpacked so I can see what I have. My uniforms are in the suitcases I have been living out of for the past week, and Lord knows, all the stuff I bought yesterday has to get put away, hung, and everything else," she said. "So much to do, so little time."

"Khloe," he said, taking her hand, making her face him and breathe. "Let's go easy like, you know, it's Sunday morning."

"Thank you, Lionel Ritchie, but this has to get done," she said. "I will not go to work with this house all upside down. Hey, where's the washer and dryer?"

"In the closet in the office," he said.

"Awesome," she said, pulling her hand away for a high five.

"Don't high five me! You aren't some dude seeing his favorite NBA player make the free throw," he said.

"I spent 20 years working with dudes. The only touching they were allowed to do with me was a high five," she said. "Old habit. Muscle memory."

"Let me lend you a hand," he said to her.

"Great, eat first, then we can get started," she said, opening bag after bag of items, and he had no idea what to do with more than half of the things she pulled out one after the other, outside of the rugs. And there were a lot of rugs.

The rugs were simple. Natural fiber floor coverings which she had selected coordinated but didn't necessarily match. The smaller of the three which had a pop of red in it, she asked him to place under the coffee table. The soft rug was large enough for both ends to go under the couch and love seat, plus the table. Beau had planned to hunt a bear this season clean the skin to make a rug to place under the table, but this would work as well.

A larger, rounded rug, with a pop of blue color, went under the dining room table added warmth to the space, reducing the echo that he truly hadn't noticed was present until the lack of buffering pointed out there was no longer a reverberation of his voice in the space.

"Nice," he said, as she shoved a painting in his hand. He held it, not knowing what it was supposed to represent, because to him, it looked like a bear shitted on a canvas then stepped in his mess twice.

"Husband, will you please hang that over the china credenza?"

"No," he said. "What is this?"

"Trust me, you will like it once it all comes together," she told him, giving him another full-toothed smile.

The smile got him. He hung all six of the paintings. Each uglier than the last, plus a new rug for the office under his desk and one for the bedroom which covered most of the floor. To him, it defeated the purpose of having nice wood floors if she was just planning to cover them all up. If he wanted carpet, he would have put down carpet.

Next, she put up fluffy, foufou towels along with little mats to step out of the shower with wet feet. Even the water closet got a little rug. Khloe went on to add matching dishcloths and plates with saucers and cups to match the rugs and shit-splattered art on the walls. She had cushions for the benches and seats outside. New, hard plastic cupholders adorned the hot tub, flanked by outdoor candles which she swore would ward off mosquitos. He knew that shit didn't work, but he wouldn't comment. In his experience, you burn that kind of crap and it draws more bugs, which brings bigger animals to eat the bugs and left you praying those animals didn't attract bigger animals to eat you.

All of it made her happy. *She lost all of her stuff and has to start over, ass. It's not much. Besides, it looks like a woman lives here.*

"I like it," he lied, partly. "It feels homey."

"I tried to match your style without overwhelming you with too much girly stuff," she said.

"Good choices," he lied again, looking at the bear-shitted paw print painting.

"I think Jethro would like that one a lot," she told him.

"Yeah, about him," Beau said, easing into the subject. "If it gets weird, him being so close around all the time, let me know. Even though he's my cousin, I still don't like a man sniffing up round my woman like that."

"Jethro? Sniffing around me?" she asked, laughing.

"Are you laughing at me?"

"Yes," she said, taking a seat at the table. He didn't know. Truthfully, it wasn't her place to tell him, but she'd rather him find out from her than to think his cousin was making a move on her. "Have you ever been to Jethro's house?"

"Of course, I have," he answered with a twinge of defensiveness in his tone.

"Does he live alone?"

"No, he bought this big two-story house a few years back, but it was just him," he said. "He got himself a roommate named Ennis Shaken. Odd dude."

"So, the bedrooms are upstairs," she said.

"Yeah," he said, taking a seat at the table, listening, knowing she was leading him down a rabbit hole where he didn't want to see the contents.

"You've been upstairs in Jethro's home?"

"Yeah, he has a really big bedroom, large closets and way too many clothes to live in a small town," Beau nodded.

"What about Ennis' bedroom?"

Beau sat for a moment and thought of the four bedrooms upstairs. One was an office, the other a fitness room, Jethro's bedroom, and a guest room. Khloe placed her hand over her mouth as the reality of the imagery she painted formed in his mind's eye and on his face. His forehead furrowed, then his eyes squinted, the nose upturned and the mouth turned down. Her husband looked as if he'd eaten a ghost pepper and the hot had snuck up on him and singed his taste buds.

"Uh-uh!" he yelled.

"Oh yeah," she said, trying her best not to laugh at everything he was thinking showed on his face.

"But! He's seen me naked!" Beau said, bounding to his feet. He started swatting at himself as if he were brushing off attacking ants, dancing around the floor, trying to escape the feeling of yucky covering him.

"He's your cousin, Beau, unless you guys get down like that up here," Khloe said, choking on the laughter.

He stopped dancing. His eyes were wide. "Oh shit, he's gone camping with Lil Bo who said they went skinny dipping!"

"Good grief, Beau. The man is not contagious, just gay," she told him. "I hope you are not going to treat him any differently."

"Differently than what? He gets on my damned nerves, but he is also one of my favorite people in the world," Beau said, just trying to make sure he had it clear in his brain. "Him and Ennis?"

He frowned, shuddered, and moved to the couch where he sat hugging himself. Silent for many minutes, he replayed in his head the first time he'd met Ennis and the stupid movies he and Jethro liked to watch. All of it made sense now.

"Beau, are you okay?"

"No, I'm not," he said, looking at her. "Ennis is ugly with a pot belly and the top of his hair is missing like one of them monks with a bowl haircut. Couldn't Jethro find a sexy dude with a six pack and a full head of hair? Why he gotta go digging at the bottom of somebody's gene pool? I bet next they want to adopt a Chinese baby or one from the Ukraine with a missing left foot."

"Well, shit," she said looking at him. "I read you all wrong thinking you had an issue with your cousin being gay."

"No, I have an issue with him butt banging that ugly ass man," Beau said. "Eeeww, what if Jethro is the bottom and that ugly man is butt banging him?"

His eyes were wide as he started making gagging sounds. "I'm going to be sick. I'm going to be sick," he said, holding his mouth.

"Beau, seriously, the man can't be that bad," she said but swallowed her words when he pulled out his phone, went to Jethro's social media page and showed her the image of Ennis.

Khloe shrank back at the image of the man in front of her on the screen, "Oh Dear Jesus, what is that?"

"That's an Ennis and it's violating my cousin," Beau said. "My eyes. My brain! I can't unsee it in my brain. I rebuke you, Satan! Get thee outta my head!"

She watched Beau scramble through the cabinets looking for liquor but only locating the two bottles of wine. He opened a bottle of red and chugged half the contents down in one swallow.

"Beau?" she called to him as he lay back on the couch, holding the bottle like it held the salvation for his soul.

"I was better off not knowing," he said sorrowfully.

"I only told you because I didn't want you to think he was trying to make a move on me, because he just wants to be my friend and have us come over to watch movies with them," she said, trying to take the bottle out of his hand, but he refused to let go.

"Next, they will want us to go to New York and watch *Sponge Bob: The Musical* on Broadway. I refuse! I refuse to partake in this chicanery!" Beau said pitifully.

"Stop this at once," she said, yanking the bottle out of his hands. "Are you upset that Jethro is gay or that Ennis is his choice?"

"I'm hurt that he didn't tell me himself," Beau said, throwing the back of his hand over his eyes.

"After witnessing this reaction, I wouldn't have told you either," Khloe said. "You are acting rather childish. Now buck up and deal with it, Husband."

"I don't wanna and you can't make me!"

"Fine, but tomorrow, how will you act when you see him? Is he going to know you feel differently about him or that you love him no matter who he chooses to have in his life?" she asked softly. "He accepted your choice, and I am probably going to be the local circus show in these parts. Just think, there are others reacting the same way to the news of our wedding. Pretending to throw up. Thinking I'm ugly and look like a monkey or a baboon. Praying for you at the thought of you sticking your red-blooded all-American cock in my black body."

"What?" he said sitting up on the couch.

"See, sounds really ugly when it's applied to your life choices," she told him.

"This is different," Beau said.

"How is that?" Khloe wanted to know.

"Ennis looks like an actual baboon with a bad haircut, and he's having butt sex with my cousin!" Beau said. "Gimme back my bottle of reality shifter."

"Keep your ear to the ground, Hubby, you are going to learn a great deal about the people you call family and friends," she said. "I'm grabbing a shower and getting ready for work in the morning."

She left him on the couch sitting in his pity and emotions. Between processing her words and Ennis touching his cousin, his stomach had soured. Times had changed. He didn't have an issue with the possibility of Jethro loving men, he just couldn't stomach the idea of him loving *that* man. Ennis Shaken was as ugly on the inside as he was on the outer edges. It's wasn't the gay thing. Or a black thing. Surely people didn't have those feelings about Black people?

Khloe was a Montgomery. The name stood for something in these parts. Either they would accept his wife and treat her with respect, or he would cut off their cable and internet service.

Technically, he couldn't do that. It was unethical. He could interrupt services for a day or three, though. The thought made him feel better as he also prepared himself for his work week.

Chapter Fourteen – Well, That's Just Plain Nasty

M*onday, Harbuck Tennessee*

Excitement buzzed through Khloe's body like currents of electricity as she pulled in front of the small doctor's office, seeing a dedicated sign in front of a parking space which read Nurse Montgomery. *I have assigned parking. This is either going to be really interesting or I'm going to truly hate it.* A truck horn tooted from her husband's truck, who parked in the same block, two buildings over. Harbuck wasn't really a town, but more like a strip of buildings in the middle of the countryside. A traveler could stop, grab a bite to eat, drink, fuel up and keep it moving. Today she felt the same way, but this was her new job at the new office and the new life she desperately wanted. *Now you have it, Khloe. Let's do this!*

She didn't have keys get into the building, but it appeared as if two people were already inside. Khloe opened the door, and the tiny little bell above the frame jangled, announcing her arrival. Jethro stepped out of the back room with a dark-haired young woman, with large glasses, a pug nose, and an enlarged bottom lip.

"Morning, Nurse Montgomery, this here's Amber Rae Thomas, your Office Assistant," he said. "She is highly skilled to handle your office operations. Ms. Thomas has a certificate in Medical Office Administration from one of them fancy two-year schools where everybody wears a uniform."

"Good morning to you both," Khloe said.

Before she could get in another word, Jethro kept talking. "When the doctor left two years ago, I removed all the medical files and had them stored in the warehouse. They are back now, and today, Ms. Thomas will get them all set up," he said, walking about the space.

"There are two exam rooms, a storage room, a private bathroom for you and Ms. Thomas, and a public one up front," he said. "Your first supplies for cleaning were on the city. Anything else you want or need, you have to buy and I'll see about getting you reimbursed."

"Jethro, can you slow down a bit?" Khloe asked.

"Sorry, I can't. I have loads to do today, and this is first on my list," he said, tossing her the keys. "This is the only set. Ain't nowhere about to make a copy, so hold on to those for dear life. Ms. Thomas doesn't have a set."

"Thanks, I think," Khloe said.

"Your license to issue medications and prescriptions and vaccinations will not be valid until Thursday. Please don't prick, stick, or tongue flick anyone until then; however, you can tend to the normal bruises, cuts, and abrasions until that time," he said, moving about the space. "The medical safe is under lock and key until Thursday so you are not tempted to do something which can get us all sued."

"Jethro, really, this is not my first rodeo," she told him.

"Any rodeo has the ability to kill the rider and the messenger and break the horse's leg. We don't want to take any chances here," he told her.

The doorbell jangled as Beau came through the door. His gazed fixed on Jethro who stood close by his wife. Too damned close for his comfort, but before he said anything, he spotted the young woman.

"Morning," he said. "Who are you?"

"I'm Amber Rae, Nurse Montgomery's Office Manager," she told him trying to give the huge bear of a man a smile. It came across as the young woman having a severe case of constipation.

"I'm Beau Montgomery, Nurse Khloe's husband," he replied, not even attempting to be friendly to the woman.

"Pleased to meet you," Amber said, looking at Khloe, then at Beau, back to Khloe and at Beau again.

"Beau," Jethro said. "We're having smothered pork chops on Friday night with Cheddar Bay biscuits. Will you and Khloe come to dinner? I have a copy of Sunset Boulevard I can't wait to show."

"No," Beau said flatly, but it was drowned out by Khloe's cheerful "yes."

"We'd love to come, Jethro. It will be our first adult playdate," she said, patting Beau on the arm.

"If it's a read movie, I ain't watching it," Beau said emphatically.

"What's a read movie?" Amber asked.

"One of them movies in black and white in another language that you have to read the words at the bottom to understand what the hell they're saying," Beau grumbled.

"It's black and white, and has sound," Jethro said. "Gotta run, but remember Khloe, no prescriptions."

"Got it," she said, giving him a small wave and turning to her husband. "Came to wish me luck?"

"You don't need luck," he said, looking about the freshly painted office. The idea to bring the bear shit paw print painting down here made him smile. He could almost hear the comments from the locals. 'Hey Nurse, a bear shitting on your wall.'

Khloe could almost hear his mind working. Tilting her head, she asked, "Beau? Penny for the idea in your head?"

"Just thinking how great that painting in the dining room would look on this wall," he said.

"You think it would?"

"Woman, it would look just fab," he said, making his eyes wide. "This evening, I will even load it up in your truck and personally hang it on *that* wall."

"You just hate that painting, don't you?"

"Almost as much as going to dinner Friday with Tweedle Dee and Tweedle Ugly," he said.

"That is not nice, judging the man based on his looks," Khloe said in a low whisper.

"I'm not!" Beau declared. "He's ugly on the inside, too. You'll see what I mean."

Khloe didn't have time to see much of anything. She touched the Montgomery crest necklace thinking not much could get uglier than that thing. Her afternoon changed as quickly as her thoughts of the truly ugly with the arrival of Kaylie Springer and the rash that kept on giving.

"NO, IT'S NOT A SEXUALLY transmitted disease, Kaylie," Khloe told her. "But let me caution you to wash your hands in warm soapy water each time you go to the bathroom."

"Is that why I have the rash around my mouth?"

"Quite possibly, just touching the open pustules and then touching your mouth can transfer the bacteria and make it spread," she told the young woman, whose eyes became quite large.

"Am I contagious?" Kaylie asked.

"With the rash inflamed as it yes, you can spread it to another person," she said. "I am going to give you a crème to put on it, and please, if you have had contact with anyone, I suggest you send them to see me as soon as possible so we can get this under wraps."

"Thank you, Nurse Montgomery," she said. "You're a real nice lady."

"I appreciate that, but remember, anyone you've had contact with and has the rash needs to come and see me," she told Kaylie.

The young woman took the crème, left a jar of strawberry preserves in payment, and headed to her vehicle. Kaylie had barely closed the door of the pick-up, when her husband, one Jud Rogers, bolted through the door, went into an exam room, and dropped his pants. Although she thought it odd, the man left her two dirty rocks as payment and stood on the sidewalk, staring across the street at the diner. He stood there so long, Kaylie had to almost push the man to get him into the truck. She looked at the two rocks again, suggesting the shelf in her office is where they would store all the unusual payments for services. Looking out the door again, Jud sat in the truck, leaning over to look out his side mirrors across the street. Eventually, he put the truck in gear and pulled off.

Khloe ignored the oddity, as well as the rocks, and continued setting up the office with Amber.

TUESDAY

Tuesday morning brought a visit from her brother-in-law, Lil Bo. His cheeks were red as he used his head to point towards the exam room. When she didn't move, he waved his hand for Khloe to follow him.

"Kaylie said I needed to come and see you," he said, lowering his eyes. "I'm not sure how I feel about dropping my drawers in front of you, but I'm tired of itching like I got the crabs. Is this some kind of S.D.D.?"

"You mean an STD?"

"An STD you can cure, well most of 'em any. An SDD is a sexually deadly disease that turns your tongue black and you end up with your man meat in a pickle jar!" Lil Bo said. "Plus, it feels weird having my brother's wife look at my Donkey Dong."

"If it's any consolation, you are twins, so seeing one is like seeing the other," she told him. "Make sure if you have had contact with anyone that you send them over to see me so we can get this cleared up for all involved."

"Sure thing," Lil Bo said. "You will keep this confidential right?"

"Of course, it would be unethical of me to share any one's medical history," she said.

"Good, I may be sending a few people your way," he said exposing the rash with his hands perched on his hips to display a replica of the penis she'd had before breakfast this morning. "You said I needed to send people I've been intimate with your way?"

Restating the need to send others to see her agreed upon as Lil Bo said he'd send a few customers to the office. A few people were more like six with two being from outlying counties. One, a very close by victim. Worked two doors down for Montgomery Communications.

"Sarah Jean, how can I help you today?" Khloe said to the young woman who had aided Khloe on her wedding day last week.

"Lil Bo said I needed to come to see you," Sarah Jean said bashfully.

Giving her the same crème and same spiel to bring others she'd come in contact with to the office for treatment, the girl barely made it out the door before pulling out her phone. The good news was that she had money and paid for the treatment with a crisp twenty.

It wasn't much, but it was a start.

WEDNESDAY

Before Khloe could get in the front door of her offices, Buck Wilson and his two cousins were waiting for treatment from the rash that kept on giving. Fredo and Daisy were brother and sister, and Buck Wilson was their cousin. Each of them could have been no older than 16, maybe 17 years in age, but the rash was flowering on all three of them.

Treating each patient individually, she opted to speak to them as a group. "Guys, it's important to stay clear of sex until this rash clears up," Khloe said.

"Can I use my mouth?" Daisy Wilson asked.

"If you do, the rash will get in your mouth and on your tongue, possibly making the muscle swell and choke you to death," Khloe said.

"She don't mind none choking on a muscle," Buck Wilson said in the most lascivious manner, making Khloe want to slap him upside the head.

"Until the rash is gone, please abstain, I mean don't have any type of sex until it clears up," Khloe said.

"Thank you," Fredo said trying to hide the growing rash infected erection. "I swear, we ain't really ever been this close to a Black person before. Your skin sure is pretty. Can I touch you?"

"No, you can take this crème and apply it around the outside of your mouth," she said. "Wash your hands frequently."

Daisy left a jar of pickles as payment, while the other two left a skinned rabbit and mini jug of moonshine.

"What in the hell is that smell?" Amber Rae asked.

"I think this dead ass rabbit," Khloe said, putting the clear plastic bag in the refrigerator.

"Nurse Montgomery, I don't mean to pry, but I have a question?"

"Shoot," Khloe said, placing the skinned rabbit in the fridge. She would ask Jethro later about trash service for the strip of town they called Harbuck. The rabbit didn't smell as bad in the plastic bag, and she hoped it wouldn't contaminate everything in the fridge.

"Those three...Daisy, Buck, and Fredo were all cousins, right?" she asked, squinting her eyes.

"Yes," Khloe said, giving her office manager a poker face.

"That's just plain nasty," Amber Rae said.

"Amber, we don't judge. We treat 'em and street 'em," Khloe said, getting back to work to set up for the rush of immunizations coming in next week.

However, by the looks of things, getting through this week was going to be tough.

THURSDAY

Jolene Beard, who ran the café and bar across the street and the caterer of Khloe's wedding reception, paid her a visit mid-day on Thursday. She came bearing gifts of apple cobbler and a pork chop sandwich, baked, not fried.

"Jethro told me you didn't really eat fried foods," Jolene said, looking bashful.

"I don't, but I had planned to come see you this week to bring you this thank you gift for catering my reception," Khloe said, pulling a gift bag from her desk drawer. "Silly me was trying to get up my nerve to come talk to you."

"Here I was trying to get up mine to come talk to you too, Hun," Jolene said.

"So, what do we do now?" Khloe asked.

"You can start by treating this rash on my cooch," Jolene said. "My husband Rock is gonna come later, but man this is a mess. So many folks with this damned rash. It must be in the water."

"Just make sure you're using warm soapy water each time you touch the infected area," Khloe said, offering a carefully crafted smile, which felt far from natural. After Jolene departed, she looked at the pork chop and apple cobbler.

"I ain't eating it," Amber Rae said.

"That makes two of us," Khloe said, trying to find a way to dispose of it since there was no trash service. The plus side of the whole situation was that Jethro took the rabbit, saying it would be good eating. He could also take the pork chop and apple cobbler.

"Did she say her husband was Rock?" Amber Rae said. "The man's name is Rock Beard. Lord, these people."

By the end of the day, Khloe felt the same way. Rock Beard came for treatment, then sent Mary Sue, which cycled back to Lil Bo, who returned to make sure he, Kaylie and Mary Sue all had the same strain of crotch crud. Mary Sue, humiliated, sent in the last person Khloe expected to see, Jethro Montgomery.

"Please don't mention this to Beau. He warned me about Mary Sue, but when the bear needs his honey, he goes to the source," Jethro said. "That little lady sure is sweet."

"I can imagine," she said. "Is there anyone else you have come into contact with who needs to be treated?"

"No, just Mary Sue and Jolene," he said, lowering his head.

"Well, that answers that question," she said, giving him a smile as she checked his inner thighs.

"Good. Good. This is embarrassing having you look so closely at my man stick." Jethro said looking up at the ceiling. "We still on for dinner tomorrow night at my place?"

"Of course, I'm looking forward to it," Khloe said, turning her back as he pulled up his trousers.

The room was quiet as she made notes in his chart which was thin in comparison to Mary Sue's, who by the looks of the thickness of the record, was a frequent visitor in the doctor's office. She reminded him that he'd need a tetanus shot soon and once more asked if there was anything she needed to bring for dinner the next day.

"I have everything," he said softly and cleared his throat as if he were about to start a new paragraph in the conversation. "He almost didn't write the ad."

"Who are we talking about, Jethro?"

"Beau. Mr. Lucky," Jethro said. "Leave it to him to place an ad on Tuesday and be married in the next two weeks. Here you are, bright as a shiny button in the summer sun, and lovely to boot. He is lucky."

"It is my firm belief that I am the lucky one, Jethro," she said. "I not only married a good man, but I inherited a good family as well."

He nodded his head, tapped at the imaginary brim of his hat, and left. Khloe was ready to lock up as and call it a night, but Amber wandered in, her head hung low. She knew the look.

"Come on, let me examine you," Khloe said gently as she would to a child with a broken arm.

"We wore protection," Amber Rae said, "but I started itching yesterday and now my skin is all red and blotchy."

"It's just a horrible yeast infection. Don't fret, Nurse Montgomery will take care of you," Khloe said to the woman as she took a look at just another vajayjay in a long week. She didn't know how her mother did this for a living her entire career. This was only number six in five days. *I am the only medical professional in these parts in two years.* Sighing deeply, she prepared herself mentally for the challenges to come not only as the wife of Beauregard Montgomery, but as also, quite possibly, the only Black woman for 100 miles.

"Don't fret, Nurse Montgomery got you, everything will be just fine," she said to herself, and for the first time in her life, she believed it.

Chapter Fifteen – Dinner and Show and a visit from Honey

The smile was permanently frozen on Khloe's face after she took a look at one Ennis Shaken. Never in her life had she seen such an odd-looking human who seriously looked as if Dr. Moreau on his island of oddities said, "Fuck it, I give up on this one."

Ennis' ears protruded from the side of his head as if they were housed in the thick bushy mutton chop beard that hung around his neck as if the hairs were confused on which direction to grow. A full bottom lip covered a row of oversized teeth, far larger than the top set, which neatly sat behind the bottom row when he closed his mouth. In her estimation, it was an underbite from hell.

"Khloe, this is my good friend, Ennis Shaken. He's an herbalist and makes a great number of natural remedies for everything for the common cold to arthritis rubs," Jethro said with pride. "Khloe is a Nurse Practitioner. I think you two will have loads to talk about."

"Pleeassuure to meet you KKKKhlooe," he said, elongating all the words in a thick Southern drawl.

The stupid smile would not move, even when she spoke, "Ennis, how nice to meet you," she said, looking at Beau.

Beau stared at her and the uncharacteristic smile that she had stuck in *oh shit* mode. He nudged her with his elbow. The smile still stayed.

"What's with the smile?" Beau asked as they followed Jethro into the large home.

"I can't make it stop," she said through clenched teeth. "I'm trying to close my mouth, but I think it's frozen in place."

"Try harder, you look like a crazy woman," Beau said.

"I'm trying but he's scaring me," she said.

"Told you he was ugly," Beau countered.

"He's not ugly, just...oh my God," she said, looking at the man from the back, "he has a huge ass."

"That ain't all, just wait until he sits down," Beau said, frowning.

Jethro dragged them all into the great room, where four large chairs faced the center of the room. Ennis took a seat in the chair furthest from the group. His six-four frame loaded with misplaced bulk plunked down in the chair. He offered everyone in the room a bird's eye view of his man spread and Khloe nearly gasped. Averting her eyes from the giant imprint of the largest penis she'd ever seen in her life, the smile almost turned into a sorrowful cry at the thought of any woman wrestling with Ennis.

"Stop staring at his cock, Khloe," Beau whispered.

"It's like a pre-schooler's leg trapped inside of those pants," she said, looking at him with the smile trembling on lips unable to close. The soup bowl haircut with the bald spot in the middle of the crown of his head didn't help.

"I gggrilled some chicken and corn on the cob for dinner to accompany a leafy green salad from our garden," Ennis said to them.

"Good, I'm hungry," Beau said, turning to Jethro. "Hey, Ennis while I'm here, you wanted to give me a couple of snips of that parsley and that muscle relaxing herbal recipe to put in my smoothies."

"Let me get that from my room," Ennis said, getting to his feet and heading towards the kitchen.

Beau's eyes were wide as he watched the man enter the kitchen and go down a hall where he assumed the laundry room was located. His stare went to Khloe who still sat, immobile, grinning like she'd just let go of a sour one. Turning his attention back to Jethro, he cleared his throat.

"Uhhhm, I didn't know there was a master suite downstairs," Beau said.

"Oh yeah, I live up and he stays down here," Jethro said. "It works out better. He can't climb the stairs. Bad knees with his condition, you know."

Beau squinted at Khloe and she read his expression of relief knowing that Ennis wasn't having butt sex with his cousin. After seeing what Ennis was working with, she fully understood Beau's outrage and need to drink a whole bottle of wine in a few gulps. She couldn't imagine trying to get that monster penis into her vagina let alone up her rectum. The vision of her husband imagining Jethro on the couch being pounded in the butt by Ennis and his Cricket bat made her snort. Then she started to laugh.

"Khloe, you are acting strange," Jethro said.

"I'm so sorry," she said, laughing harder. "At first I couldn't smile, you know, because life for me kind of sucked, but now, I can't seem to stop laughing."

She let out a loud guffaw, snorting again, then looked at Beau who had squinted his eyes at her, only making her laugh harder.

"Well, good for you," Jethro said, as he watched her slide down in the chair, holding her side. The laughter getting louder, morphing from chuckles, to guffaws and finally more snorts as she tried to catch her breath.

Beau was not amused. "I'm so mad at you right now," he said to her. "To make me think...the two of them...just dammit, Woman."

His words only made her laugh harder. Ennis returned to the room, not really walking, but lumbering Quasi Modo style, and Khloe completely lost it.

"Dammit Khloe, you will either have to let us in on the joke or I will have to ask you to leave," Jethro said as Ennis stood still, his bottom teeth jutting out, the lazy eye almost being heard making staccato movements as it tried to communicate with his good one, making the man look like a confused baboon. She thought about Beau saying he looked like a baboon and right now, he did. Khloe tried to catch her breath, but the more she tried, the more she laughed. In between her howls, she asked for the bathroom, terrified she was about to wet herself. However, Jethro, now insulted. asked one more time, this time more firmly.

"Khloe, you will tell us what is so damned funny or you and Beau will have to leave our home," Jethro said, standing protectively in front of his pal. Ennis held the withered parsley in his huge hand along with a jar of green mushed herbs. The look of hurt on his face appearing indistinguishable from the oddity that masqueraded as a facial expression.

"Beau thought you and Ennis were lovers," she said, howling louder. "It's my fault. I was messing with him, and oh God, I have to pee."

Jethro was staring at Beau as well as Ennis.

"What? I never knew there was a downstairs bedroom, so I thought," he said. "Never mind. Can we eat?"

"I don't know which of the two of you are worse, that damned wife of yours or you," Jethro said, his hand perched on his hip. "To think! You thought I was gay! And sleeping with Ennis!"

Ennis looked at him with large, sad, puppy dog eyes, "I don't like men. A woman would do me just fine, but I am rather large, so finding one who wants to play is difficult."

"Man, I understand far better than you know," Beau said, getting to his feet. "I hope this has caused no harm."

Ennis took it in a lumbered stride. Jethro wasn't as easily appeased. He held his tongue all through dinner and changed his mind on the movie, offering the excuse he had to be up early in the morning. Khloe, whose smile had changed from one of fear to sheer happiness, gave him a huge hug.

"Thank you for a wonderful evening and helping me find a reason to smile again," she told Jethro, placing a feathery kiss on his cheek. "You are an amazing dude. I truly like you. I hope we can be friends."

"How can that happen Ms. Khloe when you told Beau you thought I was gay?"

She pulled him to the side. "No, I didn't tell him you were gay, I only implied that if he only saw one bed, that there was the possibility you two were sharing it. Honestly, it was in your defense because he was getting all Neanderthal about you coming around and wanting to be my friend. I figured, if he didn't see you as a threat, that we could become good friends."

Jethro frowned at her. "That was your strategy?"

"It was stupid, but it worked," she said. "He was highly upset that Ennis could be hurting you. Now I see why, which is what made me laugh so hard at the visual which had gotten stuck in his head. Beau loves you and became all protective."

"He did?" Jethro asked wide eyed like a child being told Santa got his letter.

"Yes Jethro, he did," she told him. "Even if you were gay, Beau didn't care; he was only concerned about you being hurt."

"I'm not going to thank you for any of that," he said.

"Again, my apologies," she said. "Thank you for dinner, it was lovely. I look forward to returning the favor and having you two over to our place, if you find it in your heart to forgive me."

Khloe didn't wait for an answer, but joined her husband in the truck. He asked if everything was okay, and she nodded it was, but Beau was quiet. The kind of quiet which made her stare out the window into the dark of night. As black as the evening had turned, she could barely see past the beam of the headlights.

"That was fucked up," Beau said. "You laughing like a mad woman, grinning like someone had slipped you a hit of crazy juice. What the hell, Khloe?"

"Beau, in my defense, all I kept seeing was you imagining Jethro on the couch being pummeled by that pre-schooler leg. It all made sense and it was just funny to me. I'm so sorry," she said. "I also apologized to Jethro."

"The good news was that you were smiling," he said. "Ennis thought you were laughing at him."

"I laughed because it felt good to not take life so seriously for once," she said to her husband. "I can be happy here."

"Tell me that tomorrow after cutting up and preserving the rest of those vegetables for next weekend's Autumn Equinox Festival," he said to her.

"I can do it," she said.

"I just bet you can," he replied, keeping his eyes on the dark roads as he drove them home.

BEAU WOKE SLOWLY, RELISHING in the feel of his woman in bed next to the mass of his body. A hungry body urged him to wake her up so he could take his time making love to her until her nails dug into his flesh. The sense of selfishness overcame him as large arms wrapped around her thin frame, pulling her close, inhaling the coconut oils in her hair and on her skin. Everyone had spent time with her it seemed except for him. She was the talk of the town and people called him every day, sharing interesting facts and tidbits about his wife that he didn't even know. Yet, pride filled him as he got to know his wife through the words of others.

The second thing that made him feel protectively selfish was all the people who'd gone to the office to see her for medical reasons. Even his brother. The comment about her touching Lil Bo's junk didn't set well with him, let alone the thought of her touching every Tom's dick that was hairy made the tattoos on his arm feel as if they were coming alive on his skin. His dick was the only one he wanted her to touch for the rest of her life, but it was a stupid idea.

Khloe was a medical professional. It was her job to provide medical care for his family, friends, and neighbors. Even the ones he didn't like or their dicks.

"I'm awake," she whispered, pushing her warm butt cheeks against the base of his belly.

"Me too," he said.

"Care to do anything about it?" she asked.

"I care to do a lot of things this morning, Woman," he said, lifting the tail of her night gown. Thick fingers ran across her hips, tugging at the waistband of her panties until they were below her knees. Using his toes, he hooked the digits into the fabric, pushing them down her ankles while he gently shifted her legs open so his fingers could explore.

Slick and ready, he took aim, giving a slight sigh of pleasure as he pressed himself into the snug fit. Khloe moaned in delight as she pressed her hips backwards into him. Her leg lifted, giving him access to go deeper. Seeing no need to disappoint the lady, he gave her what she needed, himself included as he brought them both to lusty finish. He held her close, still inside of the walls, not wanting to leave.

"You make such sweet love," she told him.

"Because you are a sweet woman who deserves nothing less," he said.

"Beau, I'm really starting to like you," she whispered.

"I'm liking you a helluva lot too," he said, rubbing his hand down her slim thigh. "More and more each second, woman."

They lay in bed for the next thirty minutes, chatting about the day and what needed to be accomplished, as well as pulling the last harvest. In the evenings, they had been canning, and much of the garden was empty. He smiled at the idea of her boasting that if she says she could do a thing, she could do a thing.

She should have included wrapping a big burly man around her pinky finger. That thing, the woman had done easily not only to him, but others. He considered himself a lucky man until he heard a tap at the glass outer door.

"Cover up," he said, as he got to his feet.

Grateful for the curtains she'd hung for their privacy, he pulled back the edge to peer out and see his parents. "What in the hell?" he mumbled as he pointed to the other door. His mother happily moved across the deck to enter through the main room. Beau, in his boxers, his face laced with concern gawked at them. "Everything okay?"

"We heard there was some flooding up at the dam and thought we'd come help with the last of the harvest, take whatever you have ready up to the house, and such," Albus said.

"I brought biscuits and my special sausage," Honey said. "Is Khloe up yet?"

"I'm up," she said, exiting the bedroom door in a loose tee shirt and pair of jeans. "Good morning. I heard biscuits and now I'm awake. Let me put on some coffee."

"That would be lovely," Honey said, passing her the metal container wrapped in a cloth. The pan looked older than her. It reminded Khloe of the old tin pans pan handlers used to sift the river banks for gold. Turns out, it was just that, Honey informed her going into a bit of Montgomery family history and the gold strikes in Tennessee and semi-precious gemstones that people still mined in the area. Laughter filled the air as the family enjoyed a nice breakfast with Beau replayed last night's fiasco with Ennis, which Honey found hilarious. Albus had the same reaction Beau had.

"That man looks like a lab experiment gone bad," Albus said. "I don't scare easily, but I wouldn't want to meet him on a dark road."

"I heard he has a huge tally whacker the size of my arm," she said. "I even heard Mary Sue, that little trollop, tried to have sexual relations with him, but he couldn't make that thing stand up. Probably because if it filled with blood, he'd pass out."

"Jesus Ma! I just ate," Beau said.

"I'm just letting her know, Beau. I mean, she needed to be warned in case he came in for an exam to take care of that rash I hear just about everybody in these parts got. I think it was Mary Sue that gave it to all those men, who passed it on to their men, who passed it on to their girlfriends," Honey said.

"What rash?" Beau and Albus asked at the same time.

"It one that covers the cooch and the pooch," Honey said with her eyes wide. "Just about every other person in town has it. Khloe has treated them all. I hear one of them Wilson gals had it around her mouth. Those people give mountain folk a bad name. Laying around diddling with each other to pass the time."

"Speaking of time, I've had enough of this conversation, and I'm going out to work on the garden," Beau said.

"I'm coming with you," Albus chimed, getting to his feet. "After we finish, Ms. Khloe, will you look after my hand?"

"Yes sir," she said, pouring a bit more coffee for Honey and herself.

"We'll be down in a minute," Honey said. "I need to speak with Khloe in private."

The first thing that came to Khloe's mind was if her mother-in-law had the same rash, she would pack her bags and leave all of them on the damned mountain to diddle with each other alone. Honey's embarrassment of needing to be seen resonated all over her matronly form. The well-worn cotton dress, threadbare in some spots from frequent washing, did little to hid the blush that went from the top of her hairline all the way down her arms.

"It's easier if you just tell me, and I can take a look and come up with a treatment plan," Khloe offered.

"Well, taking a look is kind of, well, embarrassing," Honey said to Khloe.

"Trust me, Mrs. Montgomery, I did two tours in Afghanistan, one in Iraq, and one more in Bosnia. When I tell you, I have seen it all, I have, in fact, seen it all," she said. "Let's go into the bedroom where I can close the curtain to give us a bit of privacy."

Reluctantly, Honey got to her feet and walked into the bedroom. She stopped to view a few of the paintings, commenting on how the place felt warmer with the rugs. "I can tell a woman lives here now," she said as Khloe closed the bedroom door.

Taking her nursing bag from the closet, she located a pair of gloves, preparing herself to treat the spread of a yeast infection gone horribly awry. The dress lifted lightly and Honey removed the old underwear which too was threadbare. Khloe tried to avert her eyes as her mother-in-law undressed and laid across the foot of the bed on her belly. Her pink bottom growing red from having to be so personal with her daughter in law.

"Mrs. Montgomery, please give me an indication of what I am looking for or need to treat," Khloe said softly.

"It's a risen, in between my butt cheeks," she said staring at the bedroom door. "I tried to get a head on it with a piece of fatback, but that only made it swell. I'm afraid that if it pops on its own, that the pus will drain into my bung hole and make me sicker than I already feel."

"Okay, let me get a blanket to put on the bed, and a warm cloth," she told her mother-in-law.

"Can't you just poke it with a needle and drain out the juice?"

"No Ma'am. A needle will only make it worse. I have to apply a warm cloth to get it to open, then we clean it," she said. "It may hurt a little, but in the end, you'll feel better knowing it's taken care of the right way."

"Thank you," Honey said, no longer feeling ashamed.

"Don't fret any, Nurse Montgomery will take care of you," she told Honey and set to work clearing the boil, or risen, as Honey had referred to it.

An hour later, Honey was properly cleaned and bandaged, and Khloe tended to Albus's hand. He thanked her for the work and spotted the two rocks she'd been given by Jud Rogers earlier in the week.

"Hold on to those," Albus said. "A good polishing and setting will make some pretty jewelry pieces."

"What are they?" Khloe asked.

"Garnets," Albus said. "They're associated with the first Chakra, it's the stone of physical love and relationships. Ma keeps one around her neck."

"I will keep it close to my heart once they're cleaned and polished," she said, giving him a smile.

"Pretty smile. You should do it more," he told her, hefting a box into his arm and heading out to his truck.

Beau carried load after load to his parent's pickup, leaving just enough to get them through the next week. He also emptied the majority of the freezers. She didn't quite understand what he was doing or why, but held her tongue in case his parents needed food.

"I have to ride up with them to unload the truck," he said. "Be back soon. A storm is coming and we have to play it safe."

"Should I ride up with you, just in case the storm breaks before you get back?"

"Naw, this won't take long. Storms a ways out," he said confidently.

An hour and a half later, his confidence was shot as the storm broke along with the dam, snapping the levies and sending gallons of water pouring into the valley. The hunting hexagon of a lodge was directly in its path, along with poisonous snakes and creatures of all sizes that would wash up on his deck. From high in the mountains, from his parents' front porch, he could see the birds flying from the trees indicating the water was on the move.

"Pa, I'm taking your truck," Beau said as he took off at a run. He had to get home. His wife was alone, several hundreds of gallons of water would be rushing her way and she would be scared. At that instance, he couldn't imagine her being more afraid than he was at this very moment.

Chapter Sixteen – Hang on Beau

Three times in her life the feeling of dread had touched her arm and told her to run. Once in Afghanistan when an RPG came down on their location, again in Iraq when insurgents over ran their encampment, and the last time, she was in Chicago and a shootout happened on her mother's street. Moving quickly, she ran to the closet to get her nursing bag and backpack. In the backpack, she kept a change of clothing, her laptop, a bottle of water, cell phone, and an extra pair of shoes. Sticking the keys to her vehicle in her pocket, she hustled her way to the Jeep and loaded up the items. Digging inside the backpack, she located her cellphone and turned it on to call her husband. She would drive higher up the mountain in the direction she'd seen Albus come down and that he and Beau had driven up. That was the direction she needed to go.

The phone showed no bars.

"Shit," she said aloud, remembering that she'd forgotten to put the Montgomery Communications chip back inside it.

"I have to go back in the house," she said reluctantly, as she climbed out of the truck, running at a clip towards the deck.

In the bedroom, she saw the Montgomery phone and grabbed it and the cords. A loud cracking sound came from the distance as she held the phone in her hand, and the hairs on the back of her neck stood up. Goosebumps rose on her arms as she slid back the curtains to look into the distance, and she saw the tops of the canopies sway back and forth from the force greater than themselves, causing the trees to give way. A loud rush of power pushed over the ground as animals of all sizes began to appear from the brush of undergrowth in the forest.

Furry neighbors that she didn't know lived so close materialized and began to run. The ground moved as creatures, small and slithery, came out of hiding and all headed her way.

"Oh fuck!" she yelled, running to the glass door she'd left open and closing it quickly.

Deer ran with breakneck speed, trampling the garden beds, and wildcats ran with them, followed by a family of black bears. Up and over the hot tub, rabbits hopped, followed by squirrels, chipmunks, and furry rodent-looking creatures. The force from which they fled came shortly behind them in a large brown wave that claimed the residents of the forest that had failed to escape its wrath.

Getting to the Jeep was out of the question without being trampled, mauled, or even killed by the sheer number of animals on the move. The ground rumbled from the amount of water coming in and the only thing she could think of was to get in the tub. She yanked the blanket off the bed, wrapped herself in it, and dove for the tub as the water made contact with the stilts on the hexa-house. The foundation rocked, and the house swayed. A heartbreaking snap reached her ears as the house leaned to one side.

"Oh my God, hear my prayer," she said softly, curling her body into a ball as the second crack reverberated through the noise and the house begin to tilt.

There were so many things she wanted to do. Words she wanted to say to her husband and his family. All of the darkness held inside her would be trapped, along with her body, in the rubble that would be left of the new life she had tried to start with a large man covered in tattoos and a modified mohawk.

"Beau, come find me," she whispered as she squeezed her eyes shut and began to pray.

THE FIRST THING HE was going to do when all of this was over would be to get his Pa a new truck. This one wasn't fast enough to get him down the mountain to his home. To Khloe. His wife. The life mate he'd prayed to have. She'd shown up and married him, sharing a home that most women would not have considered sprucing up to their taste, but she did. His woman started a job caring for the people of the county and didn't balk at any of it. Khloe had taken care of his mother without even blinking an eye and now she was alone, possibly scared out of her mind, and she didn't know where to run from what was heading her way.

He called her three times as he drove like a bat out of hell. Swerving, shifting gears, and putting his foot into the floor with the gas pedal, he tried to avoid the animals breaking through the trees like the migration of the wildebeest of the Serengeti.

"Hold on, woman, Beau's coming for you," he said, gripping the steering wheel as he rounded the last bend to the clearing where the hunting lodge stood.

The trees began to wave in the wind as the force of water rampaged through the wood line toward the house. Pressing the gas pedal harder, he made the turn too fast, bringing the truck around the bend on two wheels, and he leaned on the door, trying to use his weight to keep if from turning on its side. He spotted her Jeep but she wasn't it. Animals of all shapes and sizes scampered over the deck, ripping through the screened porch and falling into the hot tub as others made a beeline for the truck. He couldn't stop. He wouldn't stop until he reached her.

The water reached the house first. He heard the crack when the support stilt broke. The base of the stilts cemented into six-foot boots couldn't withstand pressure hit midpoint on the wood, but the water hit the supports with such force, it snapped the legs of house and he saw it begin to tilt.

"Khloe!" he screamed as he reached the parking pad on top of the hill. He didn't bother to turn off the truck as he jumped out, coming face to face with a Momma black bear and her babies. He ran past her and a cougar, praying their need to live outweighed their need to attack him. He jumped over rabbits. Tiptoed through poisonous snakes and kept moving as a squirrel bounced off his shoulders. Beau didn't move fast enough to avoid the sideswipe of a buck that threw him off balance, and he hit the glass doors with enough force to knock the wind out of him.

Winded, but still moving, he slid open the glass door, letting himself inside the house, whispering her name as he tried to catch his breath. "Khloe!" he called out, as the house tilted to one side.

He called for her again just as the second stilt gave way, forcing the house to lean forward. It threw his body to the floor and he, the couch, loveseat, and coffee table began to slide toward the kitchen island. The heavy wooden tabletop that he swore he was going to bolt down lifted into the air and came at his head. Covering his cranium with his arms he called out to her again.

"Khloe! Khloe!" he screamed at the top of his lungs.

"Beau!" he heard her call back.

The couch and loveseat pinned his leg between the island and the table top when he heard the snap. He howled in pain and knew his leg had just broke. The vision in his left eye blurred as things began to get dark. "Khloe," he called out once more as the house fell in what seemed like slow motion, hitting the tidal wave of dirty water, filled with debris and God only knew what else. Shatterproof glass was a misnomer as the five sets of sliding doors around the house crumpled into millions of tiny pieces, allowing in the water and mud which all slid down around him.

KHLOE HEARD THE SOUND of his voice as the house began to fall over. Clambering from the tub, she made it to the living room when the glass shattered to see Beau's frame caught between the furniture as water began to pour in with mud and debris.

"Hang on, Beau," she said as she crawled towards him. The gash on the side of his head bled profusely. Khloe used the blanket to press against the wound as the house floated a ways and then hit an immovable object, wedging it between two ancient trees and a hill.

Lifting his head, she grabbed pillows from the couch to elevate his noggin above the water and mud while she pushed at the couch and the heavy tabletop.

"Don't you die on me, you big mufucka," she said as he pulled at him, but she was unable to move him. "Open your eyes, husband, open those eyes. Squeeze my hand so I know you can hear me!"

Faint movement of his fingers told her he was still alive, but not doing well. Khloe pushed at the couch, getting it off his leg, and used her back with her feet pressed against the island to heft the tabletop off him. He was still lodged in between the love seat, which had wedged itself into the hole in the floor. Try as she might to move it, she had no luck. She pulled at Beau again, but he was too big for her to get out on her own.

Tears streamed down her face as she tried three more times to get him out. Turning at an odd angle, she felt the keys of her vehicle press into her thigh.

Looking out the opening of the house, she saw her Jeep still in place on the high ground.

"Don't try to move," she said, touching the top of his head. "I'm getting my Jeep."

Crawling, scrambling through dirty water, debris and more, she managed to get out of the house onto what remained of the decking, the water flowing across it like an unwelcome river. Wading through the water, she used her fingers, snapping off her nails as her hands dug into the mud, climbing, scrambling, avoiding creatures trapped in the muck. It took nearly all the energy she had to make it to the top of the hill. Out of breath, but she being Beau's only hope, Khloe pressed on, getting inside the Jeep and starting it up.

Shifting to 4 x 4 mode, she backed up in the mud and turned towards the house, grabbing the gear shaft, downshifting to a low gear, making the descent towards the house. Thanking God for wedging the structure into a hill, she upshifted to make the climb, coming around the building and driving down, landing on what used to be the screened porch.

"I'm coming, Beau," she said, as she climbed out, grabbing the rope wench on the front of the vehicle, tugging hard. More water had come into the house as well as more mud, and Beau's head had disappeared under the onslaught. Wading through the muck, her vision became blurry from the tears as she dug through the mess to find his head. She continued to feel down his neck, locating his shoulders as she lifted as much of his body as she could, running the rope winch under him and securing the line.

"This is going to hurt like a son of bitch," she said, looking for anything she could find to keep his head above the mush.

Scrambling, crawling, pushing her way, she made it to the vehicle, activated the winch as it started the slow tug of a 250-pound prize. Khloe made her way back to house, holding the winch line as a guide as it pulled her husband from the debris. She pushed at the mud and water, reaching for his head, to protect him as best she could until his body was free. His face, brown from the mud and covered in blood, was the most beautiful thing she'd ever seen.

Khloe cleared away any items that would pierce his body while the winch dragged him from the temporary prison. His limp form lay immobile as the rope from the winch pulled him up the hill to the front of the vehicle. She hit the button to stop the pull as she reached for her husband, feeling for a pulse.

Disconnecting the winch, she lay him on his back, leaning his head back and opening his mouth. Khloe checked his airway for potential air-blocking threats as she began CPR on him.

"Breathe, Beau," she said to his motionless body. "Baby, I need you to breathe for me."

Adding compressions to his chest, she moved to his mouth, pinching his nose and blowing air into his lungs. She repeated it several times until he coughed, spitting up brown water, gagging, and trying to move his legs.

"That's it, baby, spit it out," she said, lying on his chest. "Nurse Khloe got you. Don't fret. You're safe, Beau."

She cried as she held on to him, knowing she needed to tend his wounds before anything got infected, but she was too busy being thankful that he was alive. Sprawled across the wide chest, her body wracked with tears as she held on to her husband. Her mate. Her lifeline.

"Stop crying, Woman, I'm okay," he said, trying to catch more air into the wet lungs. He coughed, which sent shards of pain down his leg. "Maybe not...my leg is broken and it hurts like hell."

Khloe looked at his face, all bloody as the red liquid seeped down the side of this head. She needed to stop the bleeding. His green eyes were slightly unfocused but able to see her. He could see the tears. A muddied hand touched her face. "You look a mess," he said, wiping chunks of mud off her neck.

"Yeah, but did you see the other guy?" she asked, adding a weak smile. "Beau, I thought I lost you. I've lost so much, so much, and if I had lost you too it would have been the end of me."

"I'm here, Khloe, I'm here," he said, trying to reach out but his shoulder ached. "My shoulder. I think it's dislocated."

"Let me," she said, wiping away the tears but only making muddy streaks down her face. He winced in pain as she popped his shoulder back in place. Khloe worked quickly, getting water from her nurse bag and cleaning his cuts and wounds knowing she had to first stop the bleeding of his head. Next, using scissors, she cut away the pants leg to reveal the compound fracture. "This is going to hurt, so prepare yourself."

Beau didn't have time to prepare anything before she snapped the broken bone into place. She cleaned the wound quickly as the wind started to pick up.

Wrapping the wound, she looked at him. "I have to get you in the Jeep. We've got to get out of here," she said.

Together, they managed to get him on his feet, using the grill bars on the Jeep as an anchor to pull up his weight. Hobbling, he made it to the seat and got inside. He was tired. He wanted to sleep.

"Beau, don't go to sleep on me. You have a head wound plus I need you to tell me where to go and get us out of this valley," she said. "We can't go down the mountain."

"Go up," he mumbled.

"Up it is," she said, double checking his seat belt, then starting the vehicle. She shifted gears, beginning the ascent up the mountain. "Beau, where are we headed?"

"Home, Wife," he said as he leaned back in the seat. The pain coming in sporadic waves made him nauseous. "Follow the small road until it forks. Take the left fork and keep going up."

She did as he instructed, following his directions, driving slowly. She took the left fork and continue the climb up the mountain until she came to a clearing. A mountain chalet with a wraparound porch, two large dormers and front porch with rockers waited for them as a juxtaposition against the backdrop of the Smoky Mountains.

"Whose house is this?" she asked, pulling into the gravel drive.

"Yours," he said as his eyelids fluttered. "This is our home."

Chapter Seventeen – Home Sweet Beau

"Don't fall asleep on me, Beau," she cautioned as she pulled up to the front door of the house. "I need your to help to get us inside. That leg needs to be cleaned again, and I need to put a cast on it."

"Not sleeping, just a whole lot of pain," Beau mumbled as the vehicle came to a stop.

"I'm going to need the keys to open the door," she said.

"No keys needed, it's open," he said. "This is Montgomery land. No one would dare walk into my home uninvited."

She didn't argue with him as she put the car in park and cut off the engine. Opening her door, Khloe walked around the front of the vehicle to the passenger's side. Offering words of encouragement, the bulk of her big man rested on her shoulders while guiding him through the front. There was no time to look around the new place she would call home—her first priority was to look after her husband who was fading by the moment.

They made it as far as a big chair in front of the fireplace, and Beau collapsed in it with a swoosh of air from the cushion, complaining about the wet weight. Khloe removed his socks and boots, then ran out to her vehicle to get the nursing bag. Being covered in mud from her head to her toes was irrelevant at the moment. Beau was the priority. Inside the house, he'd slumped in the chair while more blood ran down the side of his face.

"I have to get you cleaned up, get that gook off you, and start closing those wounds," she told him. "Is there a wash basin or a bucket I can use?"

"Under the kitchen sink," he said, his words slurring. He was losing too much blood. She needed to work fast.

Locating the wash bucket under the sink, she returned with what she assumed was a dishcloth and towel and washed his face and around the head wound. Her hands having been washed in the sink, she gloved up and began stitching the head wound closed. He barely whimpered as the needled went through his skin repeatedly, sealing the gash. After so many tattoos on his head, sewing it up wouldn't necessarily register on his pain threshold with so much happening to his body.

"At one point I would love to hear the story behind all the tattoos on your head and forearms," she said, moving to his shirt.

When she unbuttoned his shirt, he attempted to help, but the sore shoulder prevented him from being much assistance. Next, she worked off his pants and underwear, taking note of his body as she worked both down his hairy legs and over his feet. Removing the bandage on the broken leg, she retrieved fresh water and a new pair of gloves and set to work cleaning the skin and impacted areas. After pulling the casting material from her bag, she used a small bowl to create the material, making a solid cast for the broken leg. Satisfied, after dumping the dirty water down the commode, she filled the basin again to wash his body.

"Do you realize this is the first time I have seen you, completely nude?" She said, thinking of when he'd undressed them both, but she was so turned on, Khloe never bothered to truly look at his naked form.

Beau didn't answer as she took her time, washing him as if he were a child, cleaning him from nose to stern. Pleased with the results, she informed him she needed to get him to the couch after she located clothes for him to wear.

"Master bedroom is down the hall to the right," he said, watching her disappear and return with undergarments. "Thank you."

"No need for that," she said, touching the side of his face. Leaning down, she planted a feathery light kiss on his lips. "Let's get you to the couch, but you have to stay awake, okay?"

"Okay," he told her getting to his feet, careful on the newly formed cast. Hobbling to the couch, he leaned back, placing his foot on the coffee table.

"I need a shower," she said.

"Yeah you do," he offered with a crooked smile.

"Be back in a jiffy," she told him.

The master bedroom was large, with giant windows overlooking the Great Smoky Mountain range. The windows had tinted glass, cutting down the amount of sunlight allowed to enter the privacy of the room. Stripping to her bare skin, she turned on the taps in the enclosure, stepping inside and letting the water cascade over her as chunks of brown mud hit the base of the shower.

Her hair, also caked with mud, received a thorough scrubbing, using his shampoo and conditioner. Next, she moved on to her body. As she washed her skin, the stinging sensation of the soap informed her that she too was riddled with cuts and scrapes. Her body finally clean, she toweled dry and located one of Beau's tees and slipped it over her head. She looked like a kid wearing her daddy's tee shirt as she made her way to check on her man.

In the living room, Beau was on the phone. He ended the call as she walked in, giving her a faint smile. "I'm sorry you lost all of your stuff again," he said to her.

"It's just stuff. I can buy more," she said.

"You have lost so much, yet you came for me – risked your life for me," he said nearly overcome by emotion.

"You're my mate," she said with a wink.

"Yeah, but if I didn't make it, you'd be set for life. Jethro made sure of that when you signed the marriage license. Khloe, if anything were to happen to me, you would be provided for," he said.

"Funny thing is, Erica did the same thing," she said, offering a half smile. "She left me set up for the rest of my days. Even though she was a drunk, she took care of her personal affairs. The lady was even smart enough to keep me on all of her accounts so there were no inheritance taxes."

"Her china meant a great deal to you," he said softly.

"Yes, it did," she told him. "But again, we can get more and now I have an excuse to go shopping. This house is gorgeous, but it could use some rugs and a lady's touch."

"Just as long as you don't hang any more bear shitting paw printed paintings," he said chuckling.

"You loved those paintings, go ahead and admit it like a real man," she said, poking him in the arm.

"I will admit to loving you," he said, staring at her.

"Oh really?" she said, giving him a toothy grin. "I bet you say that to all the girls who winch you out suffocating mud and water."

"I'm only saying it to my woman. I love you in a way I never thought possible," he said. "Love hasn't been kind to me. The hurt I've been through at the hands of women I believed I loved nearly crippled me. Now, I sit actually crippled and feeling grateful for taking a chance with you. Khloe, I'm not sure when it happened, or how for that matter, since we really haven't had a whole lot of time spent as man and wife, but I'm so in love with you."

"That's good to know because when I pulled you out and you weren't breathing, I didn't...couldn't see my life without you," she said, blinking through tear filled eyes.

"Is that why you were crying over me?"

"Yes, because for the first time in my pitiful life, I actually understand what love is, not what I think it should be or how I believe it should treat me," she said. "You and I aren't about the sex, but a deeper connection. At first, I didn't get it. That night when I kind of forced you, all I could think about was getting what I needed. The intimacy of it all was foreign to my life. We have an intimate relationship as man and wife. I love you for showing me the difference and helping me find my smile."

"It's my deepest desire to help you continue to smile every day, Khloe," he said, taking her hand. His face showed his pain, and she checked her watch. Enough time had passed that if he needed to lie down and nap.

"I believe you, Beau," she said, offering him a pillow, as she swatted away her tears of joy. He was alive. He was here. That's all that mattered right now.

He placed one pillow under his leg and another behind his head and he lay back, exhaling softly, wanting to sleep, but needing to be awake to interact with his wife. She showed no fear in coming for him when he was supposed to be the one rescuing her. In his mind, she had rescued him in more ways than one.

When she said she could do a thing, she could do a thing. A true soldier. His soldier.

THE SOUND OF TRUCKS coming up the hill woke Khloe, and she sat up in the bed, feeling the other side for her husband, who wasn't there. Slipping on a sports bra and a pair of leggings from her backpack, she dressed quickly and headed into the living room to see who was coming for a visit.

Albus, Honey, Katy Mae, and Lil Bro arrived in a battered pickup truck. She found Beau on the front porch, ready to greet his family. They brought enough food to feed an Army, and they came through the front door passing out hugs and overly wet kisses to jaws, and they set the table for breakfast. An egg crate held a set of dishes.

"We recovered as much of your Ma's china set as we could, but some of the larger pieces were smashed to smithereens," Lil Bo said. "I even cleaned off two of the paintings."

"You would clean those up, wouldn't you?" Beau said sarcastically.

"The rugs and curtains were ruined, Khloe. We're sorry, but we did find this little strongbox in the back of the closet. It's still locked," Katy Mae said. "You want us to try and open it?"

"Yes, please," Khloe said, feeling strong enough to withstand the force of the ramifications of the contents inside. After all the years Erica had kept it locked away and hidden from sight, now it was time to face the one secret she never wanted anyone to know. In her heart, Khloe knew the contents of the box contained the source of blackness which encouraged her mother's continuous hiding in the myriad of bottles of rotgut. Her hands trembled as she watched her brother-in-law pull back the hammer.

The lock only required one good whack from the tool wielded by Lil Bo, and it snapped clean off. Khloe could feel Beau's hand on her shoulder as she slowly opened the box, peering inside at the two items within. She picked up the two Ziplock bags that held yellowed items of clothing. Smudges of old blood were on the ripped underwear and the second bag held a dress. The bags had tape around them, sealed tightly and showing a date penned in her mother's bold handwriting. Khloe did the math on the date and knew exactly what the items represented.

"What's that? A pair of dirty panties and an old dress?" Albus asked.

"No," Khloe said softly. "This is evidence of a crime."

Chapter Eighteen – Khloe, are you okay?

She wasn't okay, not in the least. Understanding flashed through her mind as to what the items in the bags meant as silent tears ran down her cheeks. The date written in permanent marker was thirty-eight weeks from the date of her birth. It explained so much. Erica's drinking. Her father's departure. His lack of desire to be a part of her life but to take Dorian in instead. She wasn't his child.

I'm the product of rape.

Lost in her own head, she didn't hear the Montgomery's leave or remember saying goodbye to them. She didn't remember joining Beau on the couch. He held her in his arms as she cried. His large hand rubbed her back, offering her consolation through the pain.

Now he understood why she'd lacked the inability to smile. This is what she meant by life not being fair and robbing her of joy. He prepared a hot toddy for her to drink, encouraging her to go back to bed where she slept all day. After placing the Montgomery chip in her phone, he scrolled through the numbers and found her brother. Placing the call, he gave him a GPS location.

"Your sister needs you," he said in the phone to the masculine voice.

"On my way," Dorian said, not questioning, only worrying and taking a paid car to the airport for the next plane to Tennessee.

BY THE TIME SHE AWOKE, she heard voices in the living room, and the sun had set. Her stomach grumbled loudly as if she hadn't eaten in a fortnight. Washing her face and hands, she brushed her teeth and made her way towards the voices. She gasped in shock when she saw her brother in the living room.

It had been years since they'd seen each other, and he looked good. Khloe offered him a smile as he stood up and opened his arms to her. Beau expected her to run into them, but she didn't. Leisurely, she strolled over as if the pastor was asking for candidates for baptism in a dirty pool of water.

Calmly, she gave him a half hug, asking, "Dorian, what are you doing here?"

"I got a call from the husband I didn't know you had to get here as soon as possible," he said. "Beau said you needed me."

"I'm fine," she said, actually meaning it. She offered him a seat, not taking one herself.

"Khloe, are you okay?" Dorian asked, his eyes warmed with concern.

Instead of answering him, she went to the strongbox, removed the contents and handed them to him. He eyed the two bags in his hand, his eyes tearing up when he looked up at her. "I didn't know," he said.

"I questioned so many things Dorian about her pain. I tried to get her counseling and when she refused, I went myself. Years of therapy, psychoanalysis, conversations on why my mother hated me and one day, a soldier asked me if I was the product of rape. The seed was planted, but I didn't water or feed it. When I returned home from the Army, she had changed so much. The liquor had muddled her brain and she was even more distant and different than I remembered. I wanted to cry for her, for me, but what happened to her was nearly 40 years ago," she told him. "I accepted the limited amounts of love she gave me and went on about my life. She was the best mother to me that she could be, all things considered."

"Khloe, trust me when I say that Daddy never mentioned this, any of this to me, and every time I brought up the subject of either of you, he changed the topic to something else," Dorian said.

"Dorian, there is really nothing to discuss here either," she offered. "I'm sure Beau called you so you could offer me emotional support, but honestly, I don't need it. To sit and worry if it was a stranger or someone she knew is not worth my energy. I am here. My husband loves me and I have a pretty decent job taking care of the residents of these communities. This, these bags she saved like it would be the answer to all my questions, which it isn't, will not slow me down."

"Have you considered maybe getting some more counseling, after this discovery, to help you sort through all of this, sis?" Dorian reached for his sister, but she stepped away from his grasp.

"As I said, I've had counseling for years to help me sift through my family's issues. Including your failure to come back and see about our mother. Including

Erica's excessive drinking and a man who never could look me in the eye as if I was something dirty to him, is in my past," she said. "Fuck counseling and you too for that matter. If I need to reimburse you for the plane ticket, let me know. However, feel free to stay the night or you can roll out now if you choose."

"You are being unfair, Khloe," Dorian said to her.

"Again, fuck fair, you, and the rented car you drove up in," she said. "Fair has done nothing but shit on me my entire life. I don't know who is my father or how I was conceived. And no, I'm not going to take those nasty panties for DNA testing against the national database of sex offenders. Who my father is at this point is irrelevant. I am here. I am Khloe Burgess Montgomery, a Nurse Practitioner. This is my husband, my mate, and my friend. My life is just fine."

Dorian rose from his seat, but gathered his things and made his way to the door. She didn't bother to walk him out, say farewell and even watch him drive away. Instead, she looked at her husband, who stared at her in shock.

"Damn! That felt good as hell," she said, grinning. "I'm hungry. What do we have for dinner?"

"Khloe, are you sure you're okay?" Beau asked.

"I have never been better in whole gosh dang life. It felt good to tell that fucker to kiss my ass. Him and his self-righteous daddy," she said in a Tennessee accent. "All of his life he was embarrassed by Erica, ashamed to call her his mother. Never once did he stop to ask the reason behind her drinking nor care enough to come see about her when she and I needed him most."

She shook her head as if a chill ran down her back.

"Whew, I feel like new money," she said, bouncing off to the kitchen in almost a skip.

"Woman, I called him because I thought you needed him...," Beau said.

"Beauregard Montgomery, all this woman needs is you," she said, offering him a giant smile. "Oooh, biscuits! I am going to get fat as hell on your Mama's biscuits."

"You're scaring me," he said, watching her shovel biscuits into her mouth. "You just received horrific news, you cursed out your brother and sent him packing and you're standing here eating biscuits."

"Beau, you act as if I should be shocked by the news, I'm not. The evidence only confirmed what I already suspected; that I wasn't his child," she said. "Those baggies are going to be burned and I'm getting on with my life. There is nothing I can or am willing to do about it. As I said before, Erica did the best that she could by me. I turned out okay."

"How did...as a child...you suspect such an ugly thing?"

"That man never looked me in my eyes. You saw my brother, he has his eyes. I don't. My eyes aren't even like Erica's. Going to school in Chicago with kids from families with different baby daddy's I added two and two," she said. "I carried Ricky Burgess' name, but that was all. He never owned me as his daughter, and I never truly claimed him as my father."

"This must have been tough on you," he told her.

"It made me distrust men," she replied. "For years I felt less than. My mother drank to deal with her failure to get rid of me, you know, abort me. The more I was around her the more she drank. She wasn't affectionate to me, but never mean. For a while, I thought that maybe Erica blamed me for Ricky leaving, then I thought the liquor made him leave. This is why I didn't cry over her death. How could I? We were finally rid of each other."

"That's kind of horrible," Beau said, turning down his lips.

"No, my husband, it's fucking liberating," she said. "I have no need to ever feel ashamed again for who I am."

Beau was quiet as he watched her open the foil-wrapped pans until she found the sausage, which she nibbled on as she watched him.

"Does this change anything for us?" she asked. "Are you okay being married to me now that you are aware of my conception?"

"You had no control over any of that, Khloe," he said.

"My exact point," she replied. "So why worry over shit that happened before I was born and let it ooze into my marriage and turn me into my mother. The Devil is a liar and I'm calling him out. If I may quote you, 'I want no part of this chicanery!'"

She started to laugh, suddenly stopping and looking around the new home. The high ceilings with recessed lighting gave provided a softness to the room. Wood floors shone as if little men in elf costumes polished them on knobby hands and knees. The walls were bare and in need of paintings. Wide windows allowed in tons of light and the kitchen was a cook's dream.

"Hey, I love this house. Can you explain one more time why we were living in a hexagon versus here?"

"The other one was my hunting cabin," he said. "The land of more fertile down there and has more water for the garden and loads of game for my winter meat. Up here in the higher altitude, the veggies don't grow as well. On top of that, it was easier getting back and forth to the school each day."

"Speaking of school, I am booked solid next week for shots, plus the Autumn Equinox Festival next weekend," she said to him.

"I'll have to ride in to work with you since I can't drive with this cast on," he said.

"You can ride with me anywhere you want to buddy," she said with a wink.

Beau fiddled with the edge of his shirt, full of questions, concerns and other matters which he wasn't sure how to address. He spoke softly, asking the one question that he felt truly mattered.

"Khloe, are we going to be alright?"

"You still love me?" She asked.

"Damn straight I do," he said, poking out his chest to display his manliness.

"Then we are going to be just fine," she said, moving to him and slipping her arms around his neck. "You might want to kiss me now before my husband gets home. He doesn't play. If he catches us together, I don't know what he might do to you. That Beau Montgomery, that's my husband, he is really the jealous type in the worst kind of way. Mister, you don't want to mess with him, you know why?"

"I heard he's one big mufucka," Beau said.

"Yeah he is," she said, kissing him with all the joy which had been set free with the opening of the locked strongbox. Years of self-recrimination and doubt flittered away as Beau and Khloe started the next leg of their lives together. The big house on top of the hill of Montgomery land became the gathering place for family meals and celebrations. The pain behind her, she focused on a future with a big burly man who enjoyed cuddling. Her smile became a trademark to the locals who brought in children, the elderly and family for wellness checks by the nurse who knew as much as a doctor. On late night phone calls, they chatted amicably amongst the neighbors, sharing stories they'd learned from the nurse about faraway places they saw on the internet. Recipes were shared via email on foods she'd spoken about and seasonings they'd never heard of but were eager to try. Through the use of Amazon and mail-order services, neighbors pooled their money for Jethro to make monthly purchases with his credit card. The online sales gave Khloe an idea.

Montgomery Communications, in the years to come, was acquired by a national cable company moving in the Harbuck area. The same year, Nurse Montgomery began to swell with child, and a doctor and his family moved to town, freeing both Khloe and Beau to start new ventures and a country store in Harbuck. Their wares could easily be purchased by visitors who came to the annual Autumn Equinox Festival, now held in town, where Honey Montgomery was often heard speaking to visitors about her Coon hash.

"I don't eat just anybody's coon," she often told newcomers to the festival. "You have to know how to clean 'em, get those musk glands out. Here, try some."

A nice young woman in citified clothing, begged off, swearing to Honey she didn't eat meat. She held up her hands in defense, trying to ward off Honey's advances with the spoon filled with coon. Nearly escaping, she found herself cornered, telling Honey, "I am a vegetarian."

"It don't matter what religion you are; we are even nice to that Lutheran family that moved to town a few years back," Honey said.

Khloe watched her mother-in-law with pride as she shoved spoonfuls of the horrible hash into people's mouths on plastic spoons. Honey bragged to everyone she met, that her daughter-in-law was a Black woman. It embarrassed Beau to no end, but to Khloe, it was okay.

It felt good to have a family who was proud to call her their own. She felt even better when she talked with old Army soldiers she'd served with over the years who found her on social media. Reaching out, desiring to connect and talk about old times, she always refused, never wanting to look back, only forward to her life with the Tennessee Mountain man who called her woman.

It still made her nipples tingle when he said it with that loud booming voice. However, Beau still said please and thank you when she did a nice thing for him, and in return, she graced him with warm smiles that touched his heart because he'd been able to keep his promise to her.

She smiled often and the old bear knew, it was a result of him. That was good enough to earn him special treats from the honeypot that made him smile like a fool as well. At the end of the day, he grinned into the mirror of his new pick up truck as he made his way home to a nerdy little woman, who was far from an idiot who thought he was cool as fuck.

Epilogue

Several days after the birth of their first child, Khloe made a phone call to an old friend in New York. Coraline had come to Harbuck for the grand opening of Montgomery Mercantile, even buying several jars on Honey's jam, swearing the sweet goodness would kill her waistline. Making a promise to send a gift when the child arrives, today's phone call was to inform the matchmaker that the basket of goodies made it safely to the new child. A little boy, with a shock of red hair, hazel green eyes and an intense facial expression. No matter how much his father coochied or cooed at the baby, he only looked on in infant boredom.

"How's that adorable little boy of yours Khloe?" Coraline asked.

"He is absolutely wonderful," she said, with a huge smile. "So is this basket of wonderful gifts. Thank you so much for your thoughtfulness."

"You and that big bear of a husband of yours are more than welcome. How is Beau?"

"Prouder than a peacock. He even made the crib Johnathan sleeps in," she said with pride. "How goes the matchmaking business?'

Coraline snickered into the line. Papers were heard in the background being shuffled about on her desk. Another snickered followed a loud sigh.

"Spit it out matchmaker, what did you do?" Khloe asked, leaning closer to the phone to hear the juicy details about the next lady to get herself a husband.

"Me? What makes you think I did something?"

"Coy doesn't work with me," Khloe chuckled. "I secretly think you're a witch."

"Oh, I can't tell you how many times I've heard that line," she responded running her finger over her chin. In her hand she held the photos of two sisters, so unlike yet having the same taste in men. So much so, they perfectly matched with the same man.

"So, tell me, oh great soothsayer, who is the lucky husband next on the way down the wedding aisle?"

"Mr. Arizona. However, I have added a twist to this one," Coraline said. "Two sisters came in, only one wanted my services, the other sort of helicopters the younger one's life. Real tight-mouthed kind of lady works for the F.B.I. This is going to be fun."

"Fun?"

"Oh yeah, I convinced Big Sis to travel with her mail order bride little sister to Arizona, but I added a dabble or two of eyes of newt for the journey," Coraline said, snickering again.

"I feel sorry for them both," Khloe said.

"Don't; there's no need. Love has a way of sorting through the mess to find a home. I am certain at the end of the train ride across the country, the sisters will get to the bottom of what they have been afraid to say, and one of them will be getting married to an eligible bachelor who runs an alternative lifestyle ranch," she said to Khloe.

"That man runs a hippie commune and makes his own bricks. That is not an alternative lifestyle," Khloe said.

"Yes, but it for one of them, it will be a perfect match."

Khloe didn't argue with the boss. Coraline Newair knew her stuff. She was the result of her matchmaking prowess. Saying goodbye and promising to visit when she was able to travel, she leaned back in bed. Hearing the cries of her son, she rose slowly to pick him up from the bassinette, allowing him to attach to her breast to feed.

Beau would be home soon from the mercantile. Dinner still had to be made and laundry finished. Albus would probably stop by with an excuse to have coffee a little a later and Katy Mae stopped by every day to stare at her nephew. Khloe knew she only came to decompress from the kids she actually hated teaching. The doorbell rang, bringing her sister in law over earlier than expected with a new hair color.

"I need a change Khloe," she said slumping in the chair at the kitchen table. "I want to travel and visit some of those places in the world you've told me about. I need to get the hell off this mountain and out of this town."

An idea slithered up her thigh, wrapping around Khloe's leg and gave her a wicked plan. The new hair color gave Katy Mae a classic look and the change was pleasing to the eye. Passing Johnathan to his aunt, she asked a question.

"Katy Mae, have you ever been to New York?"

"Once, when I was in college; why do you ask?"

"I want to do something special for my friend Coraline," she said. "But I don't want to send this item in the mail. If you're free this weekend, could you possibly take the item to her?"

"Sure," Katy Mae said, patting her nephew's back. "It will be a nice getaway."

"The trip is on me," Khloe said, looking about the kitchen for a useless item to send to Coraline via Katy Mac. It was sneaky, but sometimes a woman needed to take a chance.

Katherine Mae would thank her later.

-Fin-

Enjoyed the story? Here are a few book club questions I want you to ponder.

1. Do you think Khloe made a good decision to not test the clothes?
2. Dorian, didn't understand the issues with Erica. In Khloe's mind, he took the coward's way out. Do you agree?
3. Beau learned more about his wife from his family, friends and the community. Did you feel as if he had a good understanding of his wife?
4. Jethro looked out for Beau. At times it seemed as if Beau didn't appreciate the things his cousin did for him. He did seem protective of his cousin when it came to Ennis. I'd loved to hear your thoughts on their relationship.
5. Beau was a bit different from the rest of his family, yet they accepted his decisions. Would your family be so accepting if you brought home someone different?

Don't forget to leave a review. You can answer some of these questions in your review. I would appreciate your feedback on the story. Thanks. - Olivia

March 2019 May 2019 January 2020

Also Coming in 2019- A New Series

Subscribe to my newsletter for more info and to stay in the loop on release dates http://eepurl.com/OulYf

About the Author: Olivia Gaines

As an award-winning, best-selling author, Oliva loves a good laugh coupled with some steam, mixed in with a man and woman finding their way past the words of "I love you." An author of contemporary romances, she writes heartwarming stories of blossoming relationships about couples not only falling in love but building a life after the hot sex scene.

When Olivia is not writing, she enjoys quilting, playing Scrabble online against other word lovers and spending time with her family. She is an avid world traveler who writes many of the locations into her stories. Most of the time she can be found sitting quietly with pen and paper plotting more adventures in love.

Olivia lives in Hephzibah, Georgia with her husband, son, grandson and snotty evil cat, Katness Evermean.

Learn more about her books, upcoming releases and join her bibliophile nation at www.ogaines.com[1]

Subscribe to her email list at http://eepurl.com/OulYf

Facebook: www.facebook.com/olivia.gaines.31[2]

Twitter: twitter.com/oliviagaines[3]

Instagram: www.instagram.com/gaines.olivia[4]

| Page

1. http://www.ogaines.com
2. https://www.facebook.com/olivia.gaines.31
3. https://twitter.com/oliviagaines
4. https://www.instagram.com/gaines.olivia/

Don't miss out!

Visit the website below and you can sign up to receive emails whenever Olivia Gaines publishes a new book. There's no charge and no obligation.

https://books2read.com/r/B-A-KVAB-ADYV

BOOKS 2 READ

Connecting independent readers to independent writers.

Did you love *The Tennessee Mountain Man*? Then you should read *Montana* by Olivia Gaines!

Pecola Peters found herself standing in a courtroom before a judge in the middle of nowhere Montana getting married to a burly rancher with kind eyes and thick black hair - because of two ugly women. Hideous would be a correct term for how the two women looked in appearance but not in temperament, yet they had gotten married – to two good men. Good looking men of means. For a decent looking woman like Pecola with a horrible dating history, combined with the recent reality of two men physically running away from her, such an imbalance in the fairy tale is what pushed her to this ending. Today she was getting hitched. In Montana. In the middle of nowhere. To a burly rancher with kind eyes and thick black hair named Billy Joe Johnson.

Read more at ogaines.com.